LOVE BETWEEN US

A SWEETGUM MEADOWS ROMANCE BOOK 1

IMANI PRICE

First Edition: November 2022

ISBN 978-1-957989-89-1 (ebook)
ISBN 978-1-957989-90-7 (paperback)

Published by Books to Hook Publishing, LLC.
www.BooksToHook.com

CONTENTS

CHAPTER ONE

Kim didn't know why she let herself be talked into this blind date. Sometimes her well-meaning friends could be extra, hovering over her love life like a desperately aging grandmother hovers over her grand-babies. Rochelle, the owner of the diner and hostess of the local book club, had been so excited with her matchmaking attempts. The middle-aged entrepreneur was a lover of romance, but her instincts weren't the sharpest.

Despite her overwhelming confidence, she'd involved Mrs. Zhang, the local Asian Takeout owner, in her enterprise, hoping to set Kim up with a new favorite stud. Mrs. Zhang was eager to act on gossip and visit her close friend Rochelle. The two ladies, close in age and temperament, only needed Kim to mention that she was thinking of dating, and they jumped in, eager for the opportunity to involve themselves in their favorite hairdresser's love life.

Despite her best protests, she gave in, kindly agreeing to the blind date only to satisfy the two matrons. She saw them both as mentors and didn't want to disappoint them. So, that weekend, Kim ended up in the front passenger seat of a pompous man's vehicle, droning on about himself, his work, and his interests. From the moment she got in the car, the excitement she had built over a new date had wilted like a sunflower on a cloudy day. He had gone on and on, talking non-stop since he had picked her up a mere twenty minutes ago. After the first five minutes, Kim attempted to ignore most of the guy's rambling, catching bits and pieces to seem like she was actually listening to his inane babble.

Introductions were typical and so was his name, but as he babbled on in the cab of his truck, she realized she didn't remember his name. That wasn't like her, and a bit of shame washed over her, but as she stared at his meticulously styled hair and beard and pretentious smirk, it started to fade. His name wasn't really important, and he didn't seem to be the type of man to remember his dates' names anyway.

"The thing about this blind date is, I don't know too many people around here that are good looking. I think I got lucky." He smirked, glancing sideways at her. She felt like she was being assessed like a cut of meat at the supermarket.

"I see," she surmised, wondering if that was meant to be a compliment. She fiddled with the tip of one of her braids to reign in some of the agitation she already felt. They hadn't even arrived yet and she wanted it to be over.

It took all of Kim's self-control to stop from rolling her eyes at him. This guy was full of rude remarks, pretentious statements, and he spewed them all over the place as though he had no internal filter. Had he ever really been around a woman with any sort of self-worth? She wondered what type of women actually fell for this type of stuff. The guy certainly represented the definition of bad first impressions.

"I moved here not long ago. Did I mention that?" he asked, tapping his thumbs against the steering wheel. It was the fourth time he had mentioned it, but he didn't even allow Kim to answer, continuing as if she wasn't there. Normally, if guys were chatty, she would have chalked it up to being nervous. But something about this one made her think that wasn't the case. "Yeah, I moved here, and I think I like it. Real nice people, cheap rent…"

Kim stared out of the window, thinking about how she could cut this date short without making this narcissist angry. Perhaps they could go back and have an early dinner at Rochelle's Diner? Then again, Rochelle had literally bounced on the balls of her feet when she'd told Kim she had the perfect guy. Kim was able to picture her twinkling silver eyes and thick framed glasses peering at the two from the kitchen. Rochelle was always so sweet, but she was also no-nonsense, usually cutting straight to the chase. Kim felt a little bad that Rochelle was all about matchmaking even though she wasn't very good at it. Kim was at least giving it a shot for Rochelle's sake; the woman was basically an older sister to her.

Kim watched the familiar buildings as they drove out of the small Georgia mountain town. She had an odd feeling bubbling in her belly, realizing she knew nothing about what this guy had planned for today. Rochelle was surprisingly neglectful about details. "Where are we going?"

Kim's date grinned in a way that made her uncomfortable. "It's a surprise."

Instantly, Kim's stomach dropped and red flags danced in her mind. Why wouldn't he tell her where they were going? Surprises from strangers were a no-no for her. She didn't know who he was, and somehow she was supposed to accept that they were going wherever he wanted, with no care how she would feel about it. She started to feel uncomfortable, rolling down the window for some air. The window was only cracked for a second before it rolled back up.

"It's too windy for that," the guy said with a slightly annoyed glance at her.

She should have stayed at the restaurant and had their date

there. She never liked the idea of getting into a car with a man she didn't know, and yet there she was, violating this cardinal rule because she was too nice to deny Rochelle's misguided but well-meaning intentions.

Kim attempted to ease her discomfort by reminding herself she had a fresh can of pepper spray in her purse. She could feel the edge of the can poking the side of fabric of her purse in her lap, its presence relaxing the feeling in her stomach slightly. If he tried anything remotely physical, she would burn his eyes and run. Ever since a questionable date a few years ago, she always kept some with her. From that moment on, she was on edge, poised to act immediately.

They had left the main town and drove into the outskirts of Sweetgum Meadows, the sly smile spreading on his face as they wove down the forested main street north of the town. Her date began turning the vehicle off the road now, slowing at a familiar gravel drive. Kim recognized the parking lot of the conservation area and state park, housing a water museum and a beautiful set of trails. The area was mainly known for its hiking, riding, and mountain climbing.

"Why are we here?" Kim asked, her shoulders slumping as the truck ground over the gravel. Having never really been an outdoor person, Kim was wary of heading out into a secluded area of the woods with a man she'd just met barely an hour ago.

He didn't answer, parking the truck and stepping out. She followed, clutching her phone in her pocket. She wasn't dressed for any sort of outdoor activity, regretting wearing her simple leather sandals. He didn't even acknowledge that she had spoken to him, grabbing some stuff from the bed of the truck. There were only a few other cars in the lot.

"What are we doing here? I'm not dressed for this weather or outdoor activities so, we should probably just head back into town," she urged, willing to face Rochelle's disapproval at another unsuccessful date.

"I have everything we need, and we won't be out all day. It's not too cold out so you should be fine," he explained, the irritation in his voice obvious. "I just thought it would be a nice surprise. There's nothing like the trails out here. I swear it will be great." He raised his brows at her as if that was all he needed to say for her to be happy.

The guy wasn't going to let up. Kim gripped her purse tight over her shoulder, zipping her jacket against the cool breeze rustling the treetops about them. Looking around the lot at the other cars, she frowned. There was no one here, everyone was already out on the trails. She realized that her only options were to follow and indulge him or call someone for a ride back into town, abandoning him completely. The memory of Rochelle's eager face came to mind and she chose the former rather than the latter.

What Kim didn't understand was how the kind, thoughtful, spunky Rochelle knew this obnoxious and egotistical man. What had made her think he was the one for Kim? Kim could bail now. However, the disapproval in his eyes and the challenge in his cross-armed stance left her with no choice. Pride and righteous fury spurred her on, that and the fact that Kim loved Rochelle like family, and she was sure Rochelle wouldn't put her in danger.

Kim recalled a conversation she had with Rochelle about how a couple of her distant cousins recently moved into the area. This guy could be one of those distant relatives, and leaving him out here might burn some bridges, an unfortunate outcome for a simply bad date. If this guy really was one of Rochelle's relatives, it would be too nasty of Kim to ditch him right there, no matter how much of a jerk he was. It was a decision she felt unable to make since she didn't have all the information and that didn't sit right with her.

Kim followed her date toward the start of the hiking trail. Her mind was uneasy as they entered the edges of the woods.

She had to force herself to take those first steps out of the sunlight and into the disheartening shade. She figured this was for Rochelle and a small hike up a frequented trail was a small price to pay to make her happy.

The going was slow, and each time Kim got caught on a scraggly brush or had to navigate up a steep incline, she could feel the guy waiting impatiently, annoyed with her inability to keep up with him. He was blatantly dismissing the fact that Kim was struggling with the walk. A sense of resentment against him began to bubble over in her belly and she could feel the sweat start to form on her forehead.

"So, what do you do for work?" he asked, finally wanting to know something about her.

"I'm a hairdresser in town, a braid specialist," she replied, reaching the top of the incline with a sigh.

"Well, that's no good," he replied, wrinkling his upturned nose. "If we get serious, you'll have to quit working."

Her heart stuttered at the audacity, making her trip on an upturned root only to catch herself on a nearby tree. "Excuse me?" she asked, trying to remain polite.

"My woman should be at home, cooking me dinner every evening, taking care of the house and kids. She's the queen of the castle, you know? There's no reason for a real man to have his woman work anyway."

Kim didn't respond, the disbelief on her face when he glanced back at her easily ignored and mistaken for relief. She had no idea how Rochelle knew this misogynistic idiot, but Kim knew one thing for sure, she wanted to get back to town as quickly as possible. To think that Rochelle could set her up with such a man made her question Rochelle's judgement completely.

They continued in silence for a bit, Kim staring at his back as he hurried on ahead of her. It felt like they had been walking for over an hour when he finally stopped on the trail, considering an alternative marker on one of the taller evergreens.

"I know this area, let's check out some off-trail sites," he said, turning from the main dirt and gravel path.

"Is it safe leaving the trail? Don't people get lost out here?" Kim asked, staying where she stood.

"It's fine. I know this place by heart."

She agreed, unwilling to confront him here, where they were alone; however with every step, she was becoming more and more angry with herself. She was totally vulnerable, allowing herself to be led by this idiot because she didn't have enough of a backbone to just say no. After some time down the unmarked trail, Kim was becoming tired and her legs scratched and dirty from all her fumbling. The guy switched from talking about the outdoors to women again as she caught up. Kim couldn't bear to hear any more of his awful views, but she was stuck listening if she wanted to find her way back to the main trail and entrance.

"I love a woman with soft skin and long hair. I can tell you try to keep yourself up. You've got a nice figure too, but you could be a little more toned. I can help you with that and we'll get you into shape. Your hairstyle needs some work too, I think. I like my women with nice, relaxed hair. You know? The soft waves and curls like Beyonce or Nicki Minaj. Those braids don't really work for me so you should take them out."

"Why the hell should I care about your opinion on my hairstyle? Or my figure?" she asked, snapping in disgust. Kim had been reserved and polite for longer than she cared to be. The man's mouth was open, and his face visibly disturbed by Kim's yelling.

"You're speaking as if you own me. Buddy, I don't even like you and have been miserable every second of this date. You're rude, misogynistic, self-centered, and I don't see why I would ever want to see you again after today." Kim's words echoed through the trees. It was too quiet for a fraction of a second.

The guy pressed his lips into a hard, thin line, glaring at her with dark eyes. When he took a step toward her, she stepped back, making him pause. He then jabbed his finger at her, as if scolding some naughty child.

"You don't know me at all," he spat, wagging his finger. "But I'm glad you told me how you felt before I wasted any more time on you."

Kim watched as the man waved his hand at her and turned back the way they came. He stopped briefly, glancing back at her before walking away. Once he was out of sight, Kim shook her head, sighing with relief. She was glad to see him go.

"Good riddance," Kim whispered, looking around.

Clutching her purse, Kim walked to the edge of the dirty path and sat on a large rock protruding from the underbrush. She was still fuming and needed a moment to catch her breath. She slowed her racing thoughts, breathing the pine-scented air deeply as she tried to calm down.

A cold chill raced up the back of Kim's jacket. It and her shirt had been pulled up when she sat down. She yanked her jacket down and rummaged through her purse. Her phone didn't have signal out here, and she realized she would have to head back soon so she didn't lose the light. She stood and walked in a few circles holding the cell above her as if it would get better reception above her head. There was nothing. She would have to wait until she got back to the parking lot to call someone to pick her up.

Kim placed her phone back in her purse and threw it over her shoulder. She turned back up the trail and continued walking, watching the trees and movement around her. It felt frightening being out here alone, and at once she was hit with a wave of horror. She didn't know how to get back to the trail, looking for footprints or something that showed where they had originally come from. Nothing looked familiar, her head swimming with panic.

Kim made an educated guess and walked in what she hoped was the right direction. After a while she realized that she was wrong, sloping uphill instead of down. She turned around and started back the way she came, hoping to start again where the guy had left her. An hour had passed, and nothing felt or looked familiar to her, tears springing to her eyes. She kept walking, pulling out her phone again in a desperate attempt to contact anyone that could get her help. Despite no signal, Kim picked a contact and tried to call, greeted only by a dial tone.

Kim shivered, the cooling mountain air sending chills down her arms and up her spine. Her breathing formed small clouds and soon less light shone through the canopy above. The sun had begun to set and things were becoming engulfed in shadow and haze.

"What am I going to do?"

CHAPTER TWO

Malik sat astride his horse, a chestnut brown mare with flecks of white and gold in her flanks and snout. Hen's trimmed mane was dark, earthy, and slumped as they swayed down the familiar hinterland trail. It was a crisp winter afternoon, the smell of Georgia pine and cedars on the wind overwhelmed as the two carefully made their way up a particularly steep, and less-traveled, trail. Malik knew this ridge well, having lived on it for the past few years alongside his trusted mare and his two chickens – Bertha and Erma.

As the two crested the ridge, near a grove of old cedars and wild huckleberry, they could see out over the shallow rolling woodland below. This expanse of small ridges, thickets, and hiking trails lead almost six miles down to the official ranger camp where the rest of his co-workers usually based themselves. Since getting the park ranger job five years ago, Malik had become attached to the land. He was offered a remote cabin as his on-site housing and gladly accepted, rarely leaving his hinterland home.

"Beautiful, as always." Malik smiled, patting Hen on the neck gently. "What do you think, girl?"

The horse simply swayed in place, dipping to munch on some still green foliage beneath her. She grunted softly and this just made him chuckle as he sat comfortably on Hen's back, staring out at the Sweetgum Meadows Nature Reserve and Trails. A popular spot for hikers, mountain climbers, rock climbers, and paragliders, Malik felt right at home. It was a far cry from his home in New Hampshire, the warm, often humid mountains of northwest Georgia. As he sat there, watching the faded winter horizon, a rustling caught his attention and he turned, spotting a small maple within the grove of cedars. A rabbit was tearing at its bark, the peeling tree bringing back treasured, but painful memories.

His grandfather had taught him how to identify maples by the bark, one of many skills the gray old ox had passed on to him. His grandfather had passed peacefully in the night several years ago as he slept. He had been ninety years old and had lived a long life.

With a grimace, Malik's mind wandered back to his childhood spent in his grandfather's cabin in the mountains, living off the land and hunting. Grandaddy hadn't even had electricity, insisting on being a man with many skills and little dependence on the outside world, as he fondly called it. They'd made their life on those mountains, hunting, fishing, trapping, and gardening. Those basics weren't all grandaddy passed on, his knowledge of navigation, finding clean water, felling trees, woodworking, gathering, and dozens of other practical skills coming in handy when he left their home for the outside world.

It wasn't by choice, the pain of granddaddy's passing only intensified by the unknown cousins who inherited it. These skills, the times he spent, and the memories he loved would propel him to seek out his own life, his own purpose, as his granddaddy would say. So, college beckoned though it was clear Malik wouldn't fit right in. He didn't understand pop culture references, intimacy, social situations, or anything that college thrust upon him as a teenager. He couldn't believe how confused and lost he'd been - climbing a mountain would have been easier.

However, he never really got close to anyone after his granddaddy passed, something that didn't really bother him. He had his classmates and professors, who insisted he use his degree in environmental sciences to join the National Park Service. It was a natural and seamless fit and Malik found himself most at home amongst the men and women in his training classes. However, when school ended, Malik spent some time traveling, working odd jobs until he landed in Sweetgum Meadows near the Chattahoochee Mountains of Georgia. There was a local newspaper he checked for odd jobs and saw that there was an opening for a park ranger in the local National Park on the ridge.

The rest just came together and even now, years later, he was grateful to be able to recall those snowy winters in New England and those stove-side chats. Malik recalled the quiet winters, when they would often get snowed in with their supplies for a day or two. It was howling out, but his granddaddy would have Malik read him Louis Lamour westerns and novels. It was the happiest time in his life but here, astride his beautiful mare on a Georgia cliff overlooking the rolling valleys and hills beyond to the east, contentment sat in his bones like an old dog. It was a privilege to have the life you want, the freedom you need, and the independence to make those decisions for yourself.

This job, this life that Malik had created, was a different world than the one he used to know, but he'd seen some of the outside world since then. All the hatred, greed, and pain had to have been what turned his grandaddy away from it all. Malik couldn't see the appeal of the outside world and thought a quiet life in the forest might be the most sensible choice. The only thing that might be missing is a good dog and his grandaddy.

As the sun moved across the clouding sky, Malik decided to spur Hen on, across the large ridge and down into the valley on the other side. They followed the more popular path along the ridge, watching for hikers, wildlife, and signs of hunters and squatters. It was becoming more common to find homeless camps along the ridges, hiding in old caves, washed out by rains and mudslides. A tragic issue that Malik only hoped to avoid, as the wild was no place for someone who had no clue what they were doing.

Hen sauntered on, swaying as the ridge slowly sloped toward the valleys on either side of them. The rugged terrain, popular hiking trail, and upcoming picnic area overlooking the river and lake below was frequented by couples, families, and tourists. The sparse cedars, maples, and various shrubs dotting the ridge made it easy to see the horizon on either side. It made it even easier to see all the garbage strewn around the picnic area down the slope. Malik shook his head in disgust, pulling the reins and guiding Hen down the wide gravel and dirt slope towards the grouping of picnic tables and trash cans.

This was the most remote stop on the Sweetgum trails, and it was still frequently disrespected with trash. He dismounted Hen, securing her to one of the trail markers as she grazed the foliage underfoot. Picking up the discarded wrappers, bags, napkins, and bottles was bad enough, but Malik wondered at the disrespect, carelessness, and thoughtlessness of these hikers who proclaimed to love nature. They knew just as well as he did that an animal could eat the plastic left behind and die. They also knew that microplastic and non-biodegradable materials seeping into the soil hurts the entire ecosystem.

Thoughtless people were his biggest problem, and as he threw away the last of the trash, gathering the trash bag and stuffing it into the saddlebag for disposal, he spotted an encroaching cloud. It wasn't far off, and he quickly mounted up, ready to move on down the ridge toward his cabin. Watching the sky as they descended, he could smell the change in the crisp winter air. The pressure was dropping, the temperature was following suit, and a wind from the north was blowing harder than it had been only an hour before.

The report that morning had predicted a light snow that evening, but a light snow was literally a dusting compared to what he was used to in New Hampshire. Though, when it did happen, locals immediately went out and stocked up on bread, milk, and essentials like toilet paper. It was comical to him, but he rarely ever went into town, living in his remote cabin and only needing to enter town a couple times a month. Malik watched for a moment, allowing Hen to navigate down the valley track into the more densely wooded hills and bluffs.

"Malik, this is ranger station seven, do you copy?" a crackling came over his radio. It was strapped securely to his utility vest, the harness across his chest holding his handgun and hunting knife.

"Copy station seven, this is Malik, over."

"How's it looking up there? You on the northwest ridge?"

"Just descending, I see clouds coming in, temperatures dropping…"

"You keep track of the weather updates today?" his supervisor asked, the familiar worry in his voice. His supervisor, Lyle, was an older man who grew up in the area. He had become fond of Malik; a relationship Malik could honestly say he enjoyed.

"No, I've not," Malik responded, guiding Hen down the switchback path onto the main utility road below. It was a wider dirt path with clear markings designed for dirt bikes, ATVs, and ranger access. "What's brewing? Thunderstorm? Snow?"

"There's a massive system in the north, pushing south that's calling for feet of snow and ice overnight," Lyle replied, his voice crackling on the other end. "Expected to start within the next couple hours."

"Feet? This is Georgia, isn't it? This place never gets feet of snow," Malik replied, astounded by the announcement. "Are you all prepared for that?"

"Well, if you have any northerly advice, now would be the time." Lyle laughed, the sound of the other two rangers chuckling in the background. "What do you got for us?"

"Don't get wet, if you do get naked, stock up on firewood and fresh water, and the most important rule of all," Malik explained, a smirk on his face as he pulled Hen to a stop on the road, "never eat yellow snow."

"Hilarious," Lyle retorted, crackling at him. "You gonna be okay? You need me to run anything up the road for you before it hits?"

"I'm all right. I'll head back to the cabin and make sure I've got water and firewood," Malik assured, watching the darkening clouds rolling over the distant mountain peaks. "You guys stay safe, don't go out unless you have to, and make sure you put out the bulletin for hikers and visitors. No one should be camping or hiking in these conditions."

"Might have some idiots looking for skiing conditions but we'll close the gates," Lyle assured, beeping the walkie. "Maybe you should come down to the ranger station, Malik. Don't want to be up on the mountain alone..."

"It wouldn't be new to me," he replied, hearing the concern in the older man's voice. "I was born in these conditions."

"Still, you don't want to be snowed in alone and we might not be able to make it up the mountain for days..."

Malik considered it, watching the sky, and turning to look down the valley toward the lake and water museum near the entrance of the small state park. He could see the reflective metal roof on the ranger station, the stone chimney and radio tower obscured by the evergreen and mixed leaf-less spires of deciduous branches. He knew Lyle would feel better if he was down the mountain, with the other rangers, and he hated to worry the old woodsman that reminded him so much of his grandaddy.

"Sounds like a plan, chief. I'll head down on Hen and should make it before the worst of it hits. Over and out chief," Malik responded, reattaching the radio to his vest.

He turned Hen down the wider road, taking the most direct path down the mountain. When they got to the fork, leading down the established trek, Malik pulled the reins, turning the speckled mare down a steeper and less-traveled track. The path lead through groves of trees, rugged terrain, and a few steep inclines before leveling out on a lower ridgeline. Unfortunately, the snow had already started falling, the wind picking up as a light mist started to fall. It was followed only a few minutes later by small flakes of snow.

It was colder than usual, the ice starting to mix with snow as he pulled his hood up over his head. Hen's flanks flexed as he patted her, encouraging her on the slick path through the looming evergreens. It was becoming darker as they got deeper into the trees and valley ridges, snow starting to blow sideways and accumulate on the foliage around them. It was a wonder and brought back fond memories of his life back up north. He smiled at the swaying branches above, watching the horizon start to disappear as the storm intensified.

"Help!"

Malik paused, pulling Hen's reins to stop her as they both swayed on the spot. It was a woman's voice, distant but there, traveling on the howling wind.

"Someone! Please help! HELP!" the woman's voice called desperately, instantly spurring Malik in the direction of the distressed voice. Hen nickered and snorted as they made their way down a small ravine towards the footprints in the deepening snow. Some fool was out here in the storm and by the sounds of it, they were pretty frantic for help.

CHAPTER THREE

The sunlight had disappeared, replaced with gray as Kim stared into the thick treetops. Large flakes of snow began to fall around her, sticking to her hair and melting on her hands. Pieces clung to her eyelashes and turned to water on her cheeks. It fell a bit heavier and within minutes she was surrounded by a thin blanket of white. Kim could hardly believe it. She'd lived in Georgia her entire life and had never seen so much snowfall in such a short period of time. It was surreal, beautiful, and yet terrifying.

Dense clouds of a hovering storm fully engulfed the light of day. The snow fell thicker to the point that Kim couldn't see more than twenty feet all around herself. With each step she took, the snow crunched under her sandals, toes wet and covered in frost. It was a sound she had not heard so loudly before; loneliness echoed with each step.

It had grown slightly colder as Kim vigorously rubbed her arms through her sleeves to keep the chill off. It wasn't working quite as well as she liked and soon Kim realized she was trudging through over two inches of snow on these rugged and dangerous ledges. It was coming down fast and at this pace, she'd never make it down the mountain before she froze to death.

Kim screamed into the growing darkness, desperate for some sign of human life. "Help!"

It was hopeless screaming when there was no one around to hear her. The only way she was getting herself out of there was finding the trail. Regret and anger washed over her as she regretted letting that jerk talk her into going off the trail in the first place. She should have refused to leave the parking lot below, friend of Rochelle's or not. Kim shouldn't have let herself be led into doing something so reckless and dangerous and hated herself for not knowing how to say no.

Kim stopped, tired and overwhelmed, as she pondered what could happen next. She leaned hands first against a cold tree, the snow clinging to the indents of the bark. It melted under her hands as she turned her gaze in every direction. She needed to spot a trail marker, smoke, a building, or something to help her. She was disappointed, only finding the same exact scenery she had been walking through. She had been so annoyed by her date that she paid very little attention to the direction they were traveling.

Frustration overwhelmed Kim to the verge of doubting the possibility of getting out of there. No matter how hard she looked and thought, everything seemed the same, especially in the grayness. A bitter and strong gust of wind ripped through the trees, pulling on Kim's braids. Snow fell from the branches and bit at the nape of her neck. It sent a ruthless shiver down her spine. Her jacket was light, her jeans average and unable to keep her warm in a winter storm like this. Kim could manage in a heavy thunderstorm, but the snow was something else entirely.

Tears sprung to Kim's eyes and started to freeze to her face as she wiped them on the cuff of her sleeve. She choked on the thought of freezing to death out here, alone and lost. Her bare toes were already stinging from the cold as the frigid air worked its way under the cuff of her pants. She also knew there were wild animals out here, mountain lions, bears, and coyotes frequently making appearances on trail cams and local news.

Kim steadied her thoughts against the rising panic inside herself, finding what little confidence and courage she had out here. She refused to allow it to pull her under. Inside, she was shaking, afraid, but she had to keep it together. She was scared to check her phone. If she killed the battery by checking the time every minute, she'd never be able to make an emergency call when she got service. She'd have to be practical and patient, steeling her resolve.

Realizing she couldn't stand there under those trees shivering, Kim forced herself to decide. She picked a direction to her left and headed off, attempting to keep in a straight line downhill. It could be the way back to the path or not, but she convinced herself she was sure, and that confidence helped keep the tears at bay.

"Help!" she shouted, the panic overwhelming. The chances of someone hearing her were slim to none, but she didn't know what else to do. "Someone! Please help! HELP!"

Barely a few moments had passed when Kim heard a shout from behind her. The sound startled her and she almost tripped as she turned around. Her sandals were wet, uncomfortable, and had caught on a fallen branch. She struggled with numb fingers and toes, unable to free the branch from her sandal. When she finally cleared the branch away and stood up, she was face to face with a striking view.

A man with a close-cropped neatly trimmed afro, dark curious eyes, and the body of a god sat astride a brown and white spotted horse. He was wearing a ranger's uniform and looked far warmer than she did. He and the horse swayed where they stood, the man's face a mixture of concern, amusement, and disbelief. Kim must have looked the same, standing in snow with her arms wrapped around herself like a mental patient. When she had called for help, she didn't expect her luck to be *this* good.

She wondered how this was possible and where the mysterious and dark handsome man appeared from. She was sure she had to be seeing things, rubbing her eyes at the sight. Perhaps she'd already frozen to death and was seeing her spirit guide or some sort of angel. Either way, Kim stood still and silent, not sure what to say now that someone was here.

Relief swept over Kim as the man on the horse approached her swiftly. Hooves kicked through the snow effortlessly and large puffs of warm breath escaped the horse's nose. Kim could hear the heavy animal's breaths as the man turned the horse sideways to greet her.

"Miss, what are you doing all the way out here?" The man gave Kim a light smile that comforted her from the inside out.

Kim rubbed her arms again, her teeth chattering as she spoke. "I'm lost. I can't find the trail to get out of here."

"Then let's get you down to the ranger's station," the man insisted, encouraging her to come closer. His voice was smooth, warm like honey, deep and soothing as he came closer.

"That sounds fantastic." Kim grimaced, her face hurting from the biting winds. She was aware that she had just traded being alone with one man in the woods for another, but the sight of this one made her want to cry with relief. To think just moments ago she had been riddled with panic over being lost and alone.

The man reached his gloved hand out to Kim, and she grabbed ahold, astonished by his strength as he heaved her up behind him. It was a struggle to pull her leg over to the other side, squeezing the saddle beneath her with her knees desperately. She found herself looking down from the mount and realized how high up she was sitting. Her nerves kicked in and Kim held tight to the man. She had never been on a horse before and feared being thrown or sliding off.

"Don't let go of me," the man instructed, his voice warm and concerned. "Press your face into my back if the wind is too strong." He then pulled the reins, squeezing his legs to urge the horse onward.

Kim wasn't about to loosen her grip. The horse's hips shifted back and forth beneath her bottom and the saddle bobbed. She could easily slide right off and hurt herself. She simply obeyed his directions, grateful for the safety of the ranger's station he was taking her to. The back of the man's coat was cold but slowly warmed as she breathed into it. Her nose was probably red and was still numb to the touch, a piercing ache shooting through her as she inhaled. Hopefully she could thaw her nose and mouth out with her own breath.

The snow began to fall heavier than Kim could have imagined as they swayed on. It was thicker, a snowy mist forming as the freezing wind whipped right through her. It was already nearly white-out conditions and she had never seen anything like it. It was colder than it looked in pictures and Kim attempted to burrow her face deeper against the man's back.

"What's your name?"

"Kim." She shivered against his back.

"Well, Kim, I'm Malik," he yelled over the howling winter gusts.

Kim wanted to thank him repeatedly for finding her, but her teeth only chattered. She wanted to complain about the jerk who left her out there, desperate for revenge as he basically left her for dead. Kim wondered if Rochelle had realized she wasn't dropped back off at the diner yet. Would she be worried about Kim yet? Maybe she ended up thinking the date was going longer than expected. Poor Rochelle probably had no idea what had happened, and Kim couldn't wait to tell her. If she knew Rochelle, the older woman would not tolerate such blatant disrespect and neglect. She'd hunt the prideful and arrogant man down herself.

"It's getting pretty dangerous for the horse," Malik spoke, glancing over his shoulder. "I don't think we'll make it to the ranger's station at this rate. It will be safer and much closer to head to my cabin. You'll be warm in no time," he continued, feeling the violent shivering as he turned to pull her forward, into his lap. "Sorry, I don't mean to be forward, but we can share body heat this way."

Kim nodded, agreeing to the cabin, allowing him to steady her as she was hoisted back down and pulled back up. She was now sitting in front of him to share his body heat, Malik's jacket opened so she could burrow inside of it against him. She brought her exposed feet up against the horse's flanks as close as possible, the numbness of her toes mirrored by how red they were. Malik noticed them and spurred his horse onward, holding her in place. When reaching a rough portion of the path, he turned slightly and wrapped an arm around Kim, holding the reins tightly. It was much warmer there even as he turned the horse in a new direction, presumably the way towards his cabin.

Malik spoke into Kim's ear without having to yell. "This way will be less rough and downhill, away from the wind."

"T-thank y-you," she whispered, wrapping her arms around his warm and pine musk chest.

"I feel bad having my horse out here in this, but I'm sure glad I found you," he explained, easing her with his deep echoing voice. "You don't have to respond right now but I hope I'll get your story once we get you thawed out. I'm sure there's quite a tale about how you ended up out here by yourself."

"Ignorant and r-reckless men," she sighed, unable to hide the venom in her tone.

"Then I'm certainly not going to lecture you," he assured, holding the reins tightly in one hand and Kim's waist with the other. "Lots of people get turned around out here and no one was expecting this big storm to brew up."

"I've never seen this m-much s-snow," she replied, keeping herself awake as the gentle sway of the horse rocked her comfortably. Hopefully it wouldn't be a long ride to his cabin and Kim was relieved Malik was so kind and knowledgeable.

To her relief, Malik wasn't at all like that idiot that left her. When she laid eyes on Malik from the ground, he was a handsome sight. Then she was in his arms that held tight around Kim's body, holding her in place and sharing his warmth and knowledge as they walked on through the tall pines and swaying branches. She could stay there, close to him forever, feeling safer than she ever had before. Kim closed her eyes feeling every movement of Malik's breathing, the steady drum of his heart lulling her to sleep.

The snow had fallen steadily on the cabin, its normally reflective metal roof covered in a few inches of snow. Hen swayed underneath them as Malik directed her toward the small stable he had built three years ago. It wasn't much, just enough room for Hen, some equipment, and storage behind a pair of sliding barn doors. He could feel Kim shaking, the cold overwhelming for someone who just wasn't used to it.

"I've got to put Hen in the stable and get her some food and water," Malik explained, sliding off the horse's back slowly. Kim's eyes were wide with panic, mounted on the horse by herself. "It's okay, just relax and duck your head when we enter the stable."

She simply nodded, following his advice as he slid open the one barn door with one hand, holding the horse's reins with the other. Once inside he could see Kim visually relax. There was no wind in the stable and the dirt and pine floor was dry, unlike her shoes and jacket. Malik helped Kim slide of the horse, catching her in his arms and placing her gingerly on a stack of wooden crates that were once full of canned goods.

"Just give me five minutes and I'll take you inside the cabin," he assured, grabbing his extra jacket from a makeshift peg. It had been hanging there since the beginning of the winter when they had snowfall atop the mountain passes. "Here, it's a Carhart with built in flannel. It'll keep you warm until I can get a fire going."

"T-thank y-you," she managed to stutter, her body shaking as he wrapped the jacket around her and zipped it up.

"Five minutes," he promised, looking directly into her honey brown eyes.

It really did only take him five minutes to remove the reins and straps from Hen, refilling her water trough with fresh water from the barrel he'd topped up that morning. He also topped off her wooden feeder box with fresh hay, alfalfa, grass, an apple, and some leftover melon from the cellar. Hen needed a thorough brushing as well, but he settled for a few quick strokes before shutting the rough gate behind him. By then, Kim had stopped shivering, tucking her arms, chin, and knees up into the large jacket for warmth.

"Come on, let's get you dried off and warmed up," Malik insisted, guiding her from the closed stable to the small porch he'd built alongside as a walkway between the cabin and stable. It was narrow and had stacks of chopped and dried wood all along it. When they finally got to the cabin door, Malik reached up into the rafters of the porch, feeling around before he found the simple iron key that unlocked the solid cedar door.

For a moment Malik was worried about what Kim might think of his humble cabin, as it was only meant for him, and he rarely had company. The dimness of the cabin must have scared Kim because she paused just inside the door, her eyes taking in the shadowed space. Malik shut the door behind him, walking to the multi-colored and rough sewn blinds he'd put over the four windows of his cabin. Two faced south, down the slope to the ravine and well. The other two small paned windows faced opposite directions, east and west, and were framed with his silly carved knick-knacks he'd brought with him from New Hampshire.

He instructed Kim to make herself comfortable as he lit three candles on his small table, a candelabra on the wall near his kitchen shelves, and two more candles that flanked the front door. This lit up the room slightly, but Malik already knew the best source of light, and heat, was a fire. As Kim perched herself on one of the stools at the table that Malik had built, he began building his fire. After piling on some dry kindling and logs, he struck the flint and steel, causing a spark that lit the dry pine and cedar wood rapidly. Soon, the small open fireplace glowed with golden light and heat. He was going to put on the small copper kettle for some coffee or cocoa, when Kim spoke, catching him off guard.

"I've never met anyone that could do that," she admitted, watching the fire thankfully. "I'm impressed. Did you learn all this in your job training?"

"My granddaddy taught me," he assured, proud that he was able to impress her. She seemed a normal person, despite the fact that she didn't know how to build her own fires. Malik never understood how you could get through life not knowing the most basic survival essentials. However, he had to remind himself that not everyone grew up in the mountains and wilderness like he did. "Would you like me to show you?"

"Please," she insisted, sliding from the stool to kneel next to the small hearth. The jacket was big on her but she was able to secure it so she could watch and mimic what Malik was doing.

He smiled at her as he showed her how to layer, stack, and position wood so that it had enough oxygen to light. He also showed her how to use flint and steel, placing it in her smaller hands to practice with as he improvised with the rocks framing the fireplace.

"How did you layer that again?" she asked, practicing with her own small pile of wood and kindling. Her fingers were still stiff from the cold and she sniffled a little, but she was focused on her pile.

"You want to use dry, smaller logs to create a frame, a sort of cone that can hold itself up." Malik smiled, repositioning a couple of her pieces of wood so they could lean against one another and stay aloft. "See? Once secure, use some kindling in between the logs to make sure it burns evenly. You don't want it collapsing in on itself."

"I see," she assured, stuffing a few smaller dry pieces of bark, wood, and needles underneath the frame. "How's this?"

"Perfect, that should light, real easy." He nodded, seeing her smile proudly at her little pile of wood. He couldn't help but smile at her when she looked back up at him with expectation, like there was something else he was supposed to tell her. He didn't know what to say, so he just said the first thing that came to mind. "You hungry?"

"Are we going to cook something on my tiny fire?" she asked, an eagerness in her voice.

"How about we cook something over my fire instead?" he asked, pointing to the cast-iron arm that usually held his stew pot and kettle. She smiled at him, chuckling when he told her to watch her sleeves and hair as she practiced with the flint. He'd made that mistake more than once up north when his grand-daddy first introduced him to their cabin on the mountain.

"You're very good at that," she surmised, leaning back and rising to her feet. He followed suit, grabbing up the copper kettle from the table to fill it. He had a full ten-gallon tank inside the cabin, just refilled the night before, and an additional five gallons of backup in the cellar beneath the floor. He knew, if they had to, that they could survive at least a few days on what they had.

The snow was coming down harder as Malik offered to make them some cocoa and he offered her a snack. He didn't have much as most of his fresh vegetables from his garden beds were canned in the cellar. She seemed fascinated by his stock of canned veggies and took the homemade pickles he offered as well as some of the venison jerky he'd smoked only a few weeks before. The two were content, sipping on cocoa at the small kitchen table as the snow piled up.

Before long the two were wrapped up in flannel and patched blankets, sitting in front of the fireplace with their warm cups of cocoa. Malik didn't have a lot of furniture in his home, which he had never been embarrassed about until now. However, Kim was happy to get comfortable in the single rocking chair he'd built and sat next to the hearth. Malik insisted on using one of the low benches at the table, propping his back up against the nearby bed and his feet up on the second stool to act as a sort of recliner.

"You're completely at home out here, on the mountain, aren't ya?" Kim finally asked, setting the cup of cocoa in her lap. She still had on his Carhart, but her wet shoes, and jacket were hanging near the fireplace.

"I grew up on a mountain with my grandaddy in New Hampshire," he explained, looking into the fire. "I find nature, and the absence of people, comforting."

"Not so fond of people?"

"I wouldn't say that." He smirked, finishing his cocoa. "I'm just not fond of most people."

"Fair enough." She smirked, staring at the fire. "What brought you to Georgia?"

"I'm not sure." Malik shrugged, glancing up at her. "I'd like to think Granddaddy guided me here but sometimes I'm just in the right place at the right time."

"I was in the wrong place at the right time to meet you then." She smiled, leaning her head against the wooden chair. "I don't think I've thanked you for saving my life..."

"Oh, no, don't thank me." He grimaced, rubbing the back of

his neck nervously. "It's my job to help people who are lost and afraid out here."

"I've never seen snow like this here," she admitted, looking out the window as the world outside darkened into a white blur. "You must have brought it with you from the north, Malik."

He liked the sound of his name on her lips, something inside him swelling as they spoke between them. The fire burned on, Kim insisting on helping him collect more wood and kindling from the porch. He was grateful for her determination, but he also had to go check on Hen and his chicken coop. His two chickens were probably hungry and thirsty and so he instructed Kim to place two logs on the fire and refill the kettle while he checked on them.

He was relieved when he came back into the cabin, after settling his feathered friends, to see Kim had already fed the fire, put the kettle on, and had folded and put away the extra blankets and jacket. She had kept her shoes on, but her blouse and blue jeans were covered by the only apron he owned.

"I might be new to building fires," she said, tying her hair up on top of her head. "But I can cook. Let me at least help you as a thank you for the kindness and shelter."

"I'd be a fool to refuse," he admitted, making her blush slightly as she turned back to the shelves. "But I should check in with the ranger station, see if they are able to get up the mountain and get you home to your family."

"I don't want them braving this nonsense for me," Kim said, her voice stern. "I know it is their job, but I couldn't live with myself if you or one of your ranger friends got hurt trying to help me, especially Lyle. He's like an uncle to me."

Malik was touched and surprised that she knew Lyle. But he knew he had to make contact anyway, to let them know she was all right. Lyle was shocked to hear what had happened, talking to both Kim and Malik before relaying the situation down the mountain.

"It's a real white-out, Malik," Lyle said, his voice crackling on the radio. "This freak blizzard is only set to get worse overnight, and conditions are not ideal for vehicles or helicopters. The state has shut down the roads and highways in the area due to low visibility."

"Reminds me of home." Malik smiled, hoping that would ease Lyle and Kim. "But I get it. I wouldn't want to put anyone at risk and I'm positive we'll be able to hunker down up here and wait it out."

"The temperature is supposed to rise again the day after tomorrow," Lyle explained, his voice full of worry. "You sure you got what you need? You two will be all right?"

Kim took the walkie now, smiling at Malik kindly before speaking to Lyle directly. "You've got yourself a skilled ranger up on this mountain, Mr. Lyle. Don't you worry about us, okay? You worry about the folks in town. Make sure the ladies at the center have enough food, blankets, and water, all right? And have the church check in on their members, especially the elders. I don't want Miss Minnie freezing to her rocking chair on the porch because she wanted to watch the snows."

"Yes, ma'am," Lyle replied, the crackle full of appreciation and amusement. "You and Malik stay safe up there and I'll check in with you in the morning."

"Yes sir," Malik responded, taking the walkie from Kim who decided to tidy up their cups in the deep and old porcelain sink. "I'll keep the emergency frequency open and the local news on."

"Good luck up there, ranger," Lyle replied. "Keep that lady safe and I'll see you both as soon as the snows melt."

"Copy, sir," Malik responded, a smile on his face. He turned to Kim, who was rinsing out the cups and washing them by hand in the cold water. "How about some chili?"

"Oh, that sounds good," she admitted, stepping away from the sink. "What do you need me to do?"

It was almost too easy, Kim cutting up the peppers, onion, and frozen venison into small chunks while Malik secured the cast-iron pot with the oil, canned beans, and his special blend of seasoning for the chili. Kim threw in the veggies shortly after, smiling at him as he stirred the searing food into the glistening oil. They were joking, talking, and discussing their favorite recipes while the veggies, beans, and meat cooked. Then, Malik pulled out a large can of stewed tomatoes and a small can of tomato juice.

The smell of cooking food filled the cabin as the two sat at the table, waiting for their dinner to finish. Malik was surprised by how easy it was to be around Kim, this stranger that literally turned up out of nowhere. She was full of life and curiosity, and when she went to stir the pot of chili, she squeezed his hand gently, assuring him she could do it this time. He hadn't realized until her hand left his, how much they'd been flirting and dancing around their clear attraction. Malik immediately paused, realizing he was walking a thin line and that he didn't want her to feel pressured or obligated in any way to him. Malik would never take advantage of a woman. In fact, he had tried desperately to avoid women as they almost always became disappointed with him eventually.

Malik remained stiff, trying to create some distance between them as they ate their dinner. He didn't want to be rude, but he was careful with his words, unwilling to give her the wrong impression. After all, it would do neither of them any good to start something she would later regret. After dinner, Malik showed her his small box full of board games, playing cards, and puzzles. It was something he loved occupying himself with, his granddaddy giving him puzzles to solve at a very young age. After playing a few hands of cards, Kim became interested in a wooden box puzzle that Malik had still not completed.

He was stuck on it months ago and hadn't come back, getting frustrated at the difficulty of the puzzle. However, to his surprise and delight, Kim was able to figure it out within a few minutes. He watched her in a daze as she explained how it worked, how she was going to move the pieces, and when it was finally unlocked, she handed it to him with a smile.

"I'm pretty good with my hands and solving puzzles," she shrugged, watching him open the puzzle to reveal the prize within. It was a small copper coin with the word: "Congrats" on it. They both just smiled at the tiny prize, deciding to put away the leftover chili in a Tupperware bowl in the cellar.

"So," Malik started, curious about her now more than ever. The snow had kept falling and there was almost a foot outside the door, blown around by the gales that swept in from the north. "You grew up here? In Sweetgum?"

"Sure did." She smiled, sitting down next to him as he got comfortable in front of the fire. He couldn't help the flutters in his stomach at that smile. "My family has lived in this part of Georgia for a long time. I'm pretty proud of that kind of heritage…"

"I can understand that," Malik admitted, his voice soft as he recalled his grandaddy's smile. "It's always good to be proud of where you come from."

"I'm a hairdresser, you know," she explained, her voice light as she traced a finger over her knee. "I work at the salon in town, and I just love braiding hair. One of my first favorite memories was with my grandmother braiding my hair."

"One of my first memories was of my grandaddy shaving my hair," Malik chuckled, making her giggle. The sound was a comfort to his ears, making his muscles relax.

"My grandma would sit on the floor of the living room, me between her knees, and she'd braid my hair all afternoon while telling me stories." Kim sighed, her voice distant with memory. "Her fingers were so fast, so soft, that I'd just sit there for hours enjoying the feel of it on my scalp. I started learning myself when I was ten, and ever since then, I've been perfecting the art while learning new, and old, styles."

"My grandaddy and I were close like that." Malik sighed, feeling her press closer to him as he spoke. He couldn't help it as his heartrate picked up slightly at the contact. He mentally berated himself to focus so he wouldn't sound like a fool. "I grew up with him in the woods of New Hampshire, away from people and everything in the outside world."

"Everything?" she asked, looking up at him with big, sad, honey brown eyes.

"No electricity, no plumbing, television, internet… it was a childhood dream, really." He chuckled, hoping it made her feel better. Most people looked at him like that when he explained his childhood. "I was able to learn everything I know from my grandaddy and his experiences. He taught me how to build, chop trees, garden, fish and hunt…"

Kim smiled up at him, encouraging his boldness as he continued, unapologetic for the beauty and wonder that was his childhood. "Where most people's childhoods were filled with cartoons, swimming pools, video games, and school… mine was filled with nature and imagination."

"It sounds wonderful," she breathed, leaning her head against his shoulder. "Your grandaddy must be so proud of you."

"I'd like to think so, though he passed a few years ago," Malik replied, feeling her hand grip his arm for comfort.

"Then I know he's proud of you," she assured, watching the fire. "You're following in his footsteps, using what he taught you to make a life that is all your own. I know any grandparent would be proud of that…"

"Thanks." He smiled, watching the fire with her. It was a warm moment, comforting, and he wondered how he hadn't missed nights like this.

"It must be lonely..." she sighed; her voice was heavy with sleep as her eyelids drooped.

Malik hadn't considered loneliness in a long while, thinking of only his granddaddy when he did. He'd never realized how lonely he was without someone to talk to and spend his time with. In fact, up until that day, he'd considered his closest friends to be Lyle, Hen, and his two chickens. Kim's presence, and question, turned that thought on its ear.

"I manage," he finally replied, his voice a whisper. He wanted to tell her that it was lonely in a way, but the words stuck in his throat, only to be replaced by different ones. "I've always made do."

She yawned and nodded in response, her hands clutching the blanket she'd swapped for the apron. He watched her now, eyes closed, breathing steady, as the golden fire danced around the room. She was clearly tired and for the first time since he'd met her, he wanted to reach out and touch that soft, dark hair and smooth cocoa skin. She was quite the companion, making Malik question the statement he'd just made. He wasn't ungrateful for what he had but he couldn't help but think there was more waiting for him.

He could spend every night like this, curled up in front of the fire talking to Kim until they both fell asleep. Her soft breathing, rising shoulders, and warm grasp on his arm only accentuated the loneliness that had crept into his heart with her question. She must not have realized she fell asleep because she bolted upright when she woke, yawning loudly before blushing at him. He didn't mind, looking outside at the still falling snow.

"Well, sorry to say this," he whispered, smiling down at her. It was a lie, of course. He wasn't sorry and was actually excited to wake up to another person in his cabin. "But it's still coming down hard out there. I think you might just have to spend the night."

CHAPTER FIVE

Kim's eyes were only closed for a second, but she opened them to Malik nudging her gently, a smile on his kind face. "Was I asleep?"

"I think your misadventure wore you out," Malik whispered, allowing her to continue leaning against him. She realized she was in his space and forced herself up. Kim then watched Malik go into the corner of the room and come back with blankets and a sack of something. "You can have the bed, I'll take the cot," Malik insisted, setting the blankets on the small-framed bed.

"I couldn't…"

"I insist." Malik smiled. "It's a real mattress and it'll be nice and warm. If you need a bathroom, this closet door actually leads to a detached outhouse. There's a candle inside as well as a fresh container of water and soap."

"Thank you for all of your help, really," she sighed, grateful tears in her eyes.

"You're very welcome." He smiled, a comfortable silence as they stared at one another. "I'll let you get some rest. Don't hesitate to wake me if you need to."

"Good night," she told him, crawling into the warm bed, and submerging herself under the covers. He smiled at her again, setting up the cot with a few clanking bars and a canvas mattress. He laid down a heavy blanket on the cot, moving it between the table and fireplace.

Kim watched him quietly as he pulled off his jacket, revealing the long tunic he wore under his uniform. His frame was broad, muscular as the open tunic revealed the dark curly hairs on his chest and neck. It was alluring and she wished he'd keep her warm under the pine and musk-scented bedding. Kim had an odd sense of wishing they could stay up and watch the storm too, talking and laughing into the night.

She brushed the thought off, falling in an out of consciousness as she watched him get ready for bed. He blew out the half-burned candles, placing one on the small table near the bed. He restocked the fireplace as Kim yawned, covering her mouth so that the noise was muffled. Malik had been uncommonly kind and though he was a stranger, fear didn't find her in his little off-grid home.

In the morning, Kim's back was a little sore, but she still felt fully revived. Her clothing was in disarray, and she desperately wanted a toothbrush and shower. She tidied herself in the bathroom after placing a log on the fire, cleaning herself just enough to be comfortable then jumped in surprise at the bustling coming from behind the door. She unlocked it quietly and peeped out, the detached outhouse cleaner than she'd thought it would be. Kim stepped out and then re-emerged into the kitchen to find Malik hovering over the fire and a familiar smell wafting at her.

The floorboards creaked beneath Kim's feet as she approached, and Malik turned around with a wide smile. "Morning. Would you like some pancakes?"

"Absolutely. I'm starving." Kim moved closer, observing the grate over the open fire, watching as he used his cast-iron skillet to cook the pancakes and eggs. She was curious and wanted to try it out for herself but didn't want to get in Malik's way.

"I haven't gotten to the coffee yet," Malik explained, flipping a pancake in the pan.

Kim darted right for the metal pot, the familiar device reminding her of her grandmother. "I can brew some."

"So, how'd you sleep?" Malik asked, throwing a kitchen cloth over his shoulder.

"Great. I feel much better, thank you so much for everything," she gushed, taking apart the metal pot and loading it with roughly crushed coffee beans. After a few moments over the fire, the coffee pot sputtered hot water and smelled heavenly.

"How did you sleep?" she questioned, crossing her legs under her as she watched him work.

"Good, it's a comfortable cot." Malik chuckled, scooping the pancake onto a stack of already done ones. "That storm passed while we were sleeping. Not sure when, but it must have set some sort of record."

"What do you mean?" Kim darted up on her feet, her eyes taking in the whitewashed view out the window. Kim could feel Malik smiling at her as she stood there, mouth open. Kim let out a single cough of a laugh. "There's a ton of snow out there! It's beautiful…"

Kim realized she was looking at more snow than she had ever seen in her life and probably more than she would ever see again. There it was, laid out in perfection as one lifetime of snow in one night and it made her giggle with excitement. She breathed deep, opening the window gently to take in the crisp evergreen air. The breeze was freezing so she didn't stand there long, shutting the window and staring back at the coffee pot. It was already done, and Malik was handing her a cup from the cupboard, filled to the brim. Steam rolled off the surface and into her nose as she sipped the hot, bitter fluid. The caffeine gave her life.

Malik poured himself a cup and handed Kim a plate of pancakes. She poured some warmed syrup on top, and they ate together in content silence. Kim gorged herself ignoring the fact that Malik was looking at her the whole time. She was hungry and didn't care how it looked. Kim didn't think Malik minded either when he smiled and dug into his own pancakes greedily.

"I can't eat any more. I'm stuffed," Kim finally admitted, finishing two eggs and two pancakes.

"I am too. I'll take that for you," Malik insisted, putting the dishes in the small porcelain sink while Kim kept sipping on her coffee at the table.

Kim realized there was a problem with all that snow outside. "How will we get to the ranger's station? The snow's so deep."

"Yeah, it's still rough out there," he agreed, sipping his coffee, and leaning against the counter. "But we should be able to make it there just fine. It's no longer snowing, so we'll see our way down the mountain."

Kim needed more information after the day she had. "How, exactly?"

"The snow's only so heavy up here because of the higher alti-tude," Malik explained patiently, putting his cup in the sink. "I radioed the ranger's station this morning and they said that most of yesterday's snow has already melted down there. We've just got to be careful of mudslides and ice."

Kim perked up. "That's amazing."

"Yeah, I don't have a vehicle since I really didn't have a need, so we'll take my horse again. We've just got to take it slow and careful."

Kim wasn't exactly excited about getting back on the horse. She knew she'd be safe with Malik keeping her on, though. She could be in his arms again and it felt weird that she wanted that. She barely knew him and yet she wanted to spend more and more time with him. Malik headed to the door and began slipping his boots on whilst sitting on a tiny wooden bench.

"I'll let you get dressed and saddle up Hen," Malik nodded, opening the front door. "Put on the extra pair of socks and this jacket near the door. It'll be a cold and slow ride down the mountain."

Kim waited for Malik to zip up his coat and walk out the front door before she checked her hair. It was a bit frizzy, the braids holding nicely in place as she tried to smooth and tighten them. When Kim was satisfied, she wet her face and dried it on the hand towel near the sink before checking her reflection in the small old mirror. Kim looked a little ashen in the mirror so she pinched her cheeks for some color. She didn't really understand why her looks mattered in that moment but all she could picture was Malik's dark and curious eyes.

Kim nabbed up her purse and slipped on the dark green plaid coat by the door. It was cozy and much warmer than her jacket. It had a fleece lining that was smooth against the skin of her arms. She tried to stuff her jacket in her purse, but it stuck out of the top to where she couldn't close the clasp. It would have to do.

Opening the door, Kim was welcomed by the warmth of the sun. It was short lived when a cold breeze swept across her face. She didn't shiver thanks to the protection of the borrowed coat and socks, but she still felt silly in sandals. She knew she wouldn't freeze, at least. The trees hid most of the direct sunlight, shielding it from the cabin porch. She spotted the open doors of the stable just a few feet from the cabin and headed toward the direction of a whinnying horse. A path had already been shoveled out and she wondered how long Malik had been awake before her.

Kim approached the open stable doors and immediately smelled the hay and hint of manure. There he was, Malik, bent over facing away from Kim, tightening some sort of strap at the side of the horse's belly. He then patted the side of Hen's neck, running his hand down to her face and that's when he noticed Kim.

"Hey, we're all set here. How about you?"

"She's much prettier in the daylight," Kim commented, still nervous but mesmerized by the beauty of the brown and white mare. She also admired the kind features of the handsome man next to Hen. A smile spread over her lips as she thought about which beast was more attractive.

"She's quite the creature, all right," Malik agreed, bending down, and folding his hands together. "Up you go."

Kim grabbed on to the saddle and placed her wet sandal in Malik's hand. He boosted her up and Kim swung her leg around almost effortlessly. She grinned that time, seeing that maybe each time she did it, she was becoming a little braver. Kim felt a pull and then the weight of Malik hopping up behind her. He clicked his tongue a few times then squeezed the horse to begin forward. The movement forced Kim further into Malik's chest as they headed into the forest, leaving behind the little cabin.

Saying the trip was quiet would be wrong. It was loud, but in the most beautiful ways. The horse's hooves stamped with ease through the snow, crunching it flat under the weight. Icicles hanging from tree branches surrounded them, glimmering in the sunlight. Every time something moved in the trees, such as a chittering squirrel or a chirping bird, snow would lightly fall from where they leaped or flew from.

Malik's horse shifted a bit and Malik tightened his arms snug around Kim. She had to turn her face away to hide her smile. *What is wrong with me?* she thought, relishing the coziness of the space between Malik's arms. Her date may have gone horribly the day before, but she ended up meeting an amazing man who made her feel so at ease with him. Just as before, she could stay right there in his warm embrace.

It was not long before Kim realized they had approached town. The ride had been long but ended too quick as the conversation was full of interesting facts about nature, Kim's job, her life, and his favorite pastimes on the mountain. They entered onto the main road and people immediately began staring at them, giving puzzled expressions and other strange looks. Kim giggled and waved to them, some waving as though the sight of the two people riding a horse through town just made their day. It was also fun because Malik was in his ranger uniform, which looked perfectly tight in the right places.

Kim pointed out a few of the people's names. "Oh, that's Darcy. She's always going on about what she reads in the newspapers."

Malik didn't respond much. It kind of hit Kim that Malik didn't know who anybody was, having never seen him around town. She became slightly saddened that Malik really kept to himself out there in that cabin. Pointing out which turns to take, Malik eventually stopped in front of Kim's home, a small rental. He brought the horse all the way to Kim's front door and small porch. Kim slid down and planted her feet on the sidewalk, suddenly worried she'd never see him again.

Kim gazed up to Malik and met his eyes. "Would you like to get coffee sometime?"

Malik appeared to be thinking about her question. He didn't say anything right away and it made Kim nervous for asking. She piped up instead of waiting, nervous that he'd just disappear.

"I never thought I'd be glad to get lost," she joked, feeling her cheeks flush. "I just thought we really hit it off and I'd really like to spend more time with you. Would you, maybe, like to spend more time with me?"

Kim could see Malik hesitate, appearing uncomfortable.

"You are pretty good with puzzles." Malik spoke the words through a crooked smile and a flirtatious glint in his eyes. "And you're a quick learner, so sure. You take me out for that coffee and show me around town and I'll show you some basic wilderness survival skills. Can't have you getting lost again on the mountain."

CHAPTER SIX

The next day was like an odd dream. Kim had gone to work but she felt outside of herself, like she was walking on air. Talking to her boss that morning, she explained what had happened and thanked her for understanding and being patient. Her boss seemed curious about the mysterious mountain man and Kim spent a long while chatting with her about him. She couldn't stop herself, feeling giddy that he actually agreed to spend more time with her.

"What are you two cackling about?" one of their co-workers, Treena, asked, prepping an older woman in the salon chair. "Gossiping?"

"Oh, this is more than gossip." Kalie, her boss, smirked, sitting behind the desk flipping through the appointment book. "Kim found herself a sexy mountain man... that's why she wasn't at work."

"And the blizzard," Lilia reminded, working on her own client. "No one could really make it during that. Not even clients..."

"We tried," one of the regular clients sitting in Treena's chair.

"Who's this mountain man? Tell me more about that… It's been a long while since momma's heard anything that juicy."

"Oh, it's juicy all right," Kalie replied, making Kim laugh.

"Come on then!" Lilia encouraged, her client smirking as she flipped through the magazine. "Tell us the details."

"He's a park ranger living in the old mountain cabin, up on the north ridge," Kim explained, blushing. "His name is Malik and he's certainly different than most guys around here."

"You've been single for far too long," Treena surmised, nodding her head in approval. "If a sexy mountain man is what you want, then the Lord will provide."

"He was amazing," Kim explained, prepping her own client as she unbraided her hair before washing it. "I was so lost after that awful date and then he just comes riding up on this beautiful horse, broad-chested and strong. Like one of those cover images on those old romance novels, you know?"

"You found yourself a black knight in shining armor up on that ridge." Kalie winked, offering some waters or juice to the clients. "Tell them what happened when he took you back to his cabin…"

"He took you back to his cabin?" Lilia asked, her eyes wide as she was treating her client's hair. "Did he…?"

"Nonsense, he was kind, helpful, understanding, and entirely too adorable." Kim sighed, shaking her head. "We just made dinner, he taught me how to build a fire, we played board games, and solved some puzzles before bed."

"Did you sleep in the same bed?" Treena winked, chuckling under her breath.

"No, like I said, he wasn't like that…"

"She found herself a mountain man with a body like a god and the manners of a priest," Kalie surmised, making the room erupt in laughter, even Kim's. When it died down, the final stylist, Jessica, spoke up for the first time.

"I hardly noticed you were missing," she said, her voice icy, her eyes focused solely on her client's hair. "It's not like we couldn't get by without you. You don't do much when you're here anyway."

"Thanks for your concern." Kim smiled kindly, ignoring Jessica's comments. "It was a unique experience."

"I'm just joking." Jessica smiled, Kim knowing full well she wasn't joking. "Glad to know the mountain man didn't abduct you."

Kim just rolled her eyes again, looking at Kalie knowingly. Kalie rolled her eyes as well, sighing before shaking her head at the two stylists. This had been a frequent thing since Kim started at the salon a while ago. Jessica was always passive-aggressive, always talking behind her back, and complaining when she got more clients. It was the worst part about her day, but it was easily ignored.

That particular day was a full day at the salon and Kim was thankful for that. Her clients had all been rescheduled from the snow day, so today was a busy one. Between the conversation, gossip, and chatting between the clients and co-workers, Kim was also happy to see friendly faces stopping in just to check in on her. Being missing for a day in a small Georgia town will make locals panic but Kim was grateful for their concern.

She also had a teenage client that afternoon, a client eager to have her hair perfect for her Sweet Sixteen birthday party that upcoming week. The mother was a bit worried, the both of them coming in in a slight panic, but Kim soon eased them. While Kalie offered coffee, tea, or water, Kim worked hard on getting the teenager's desired braids perfect. Even the mother, who was unsure, gushed at how beautifully and evenly Kim had gotten them. After thanking her again, and offering a large tip, they left with smiles and a kind wave to Kim and the other women at the salon.

Later that afternoon a guy from Rochelle's, the small diner where all the locals enjoyed their morning meals and Saturday night dates, stopped in. The man needed his cornrows done and was willing to pay as much as he needed to. Kim could see why… they were a mess and needed some TLC.

"How was the date, by the way?" Nick asked, knowing Rochelle had set Kim up on the awful date the other day.

"Don't ask," Kim sighed, shaking her head.

"Was it that bad?" he asked, the concern in his voice over-shadowed by the amused chuckle.

"Let's just say that jerk doesn't deserve to be with any woman, least of all me," she replied, tightening one of the braids a bit roughly.

"Yeah, Rochelle likes to think she's cupid," he sighed, wincing slightly. "But those arrows of hers are cursed."

Kim agreed, laughing with the man and the rest of her co-workers about how badly the date went. After he left, Kim had just one more client, a young girl who had come in for her first braids. Her mother was so thankful that Kim made the girl feel at ease, with a lollipop and a coloring book, that she left a huge tip as well. Kim felt so blessed, but she could see the annoyance in Jessica's face as she left for the day. Kim just rolled her eyes at her back, gathering up her own belongings to return home.

It was a typical day at the salon, and when she turned her phone back on after returning home, she saw a message from her bestie, India. She was supposed to have a girls night with her and was frantic to clean up and prepare her small but tidy rental. The furniture was minimal, wooden accents, and glass or stone tabletops. The décor was also quite simple, whites, grays, and yellows accented by natural wood and greenery on every shelf. She loved her succulents and indoor plants, appreciating how clean and streamlined it looked.

Kim loved keeping her house clean, her routine every Sunday morning consisting of cleaning, loud music, and orga-nizing shelves. Her kitchen was no different, her cooking skills inherited from her grandmother and aunts. She loved cooking though didn't consider her skills anything special. While prepping for India to arrive, Kim considered what tea to serve.

She had a huge shelf on her kitchen and dining room wall shaped like a world map, and each section of the map had a pullout drawer where she could store her collection of teas from around the world. It was something she prided herself on and she was choosing a chai tea from India when her doorbell rang. Sure enough, her best friend India came bursting through the door, hugging her tightly.

"I was worried about you!" she said, shutting the door behind her. The smooth sound of soul and jazz music filled the single-story home from Kim's Bluetooth speaker. "Are you all right? What about mountain man? What was his name again?"

"Relax, everything is all right." Kim chuckled, offering for India to take her shoes off and relax.

After bringing in more tea, and getting comfortable in her cozy living room, Kim spilled the beans. She told India everything from beginning to end, leaving out no detail about the horrible date, the hiking trail, Malik's rescue, his home, and the way he made sure she made it home safely. It was all a whirlwind of excitement and expectation, ending the tale just as they ran out of tea.

"He's so sweet and fun," Kim explained, crossing her legs on the couch. "I haven't felt like this in a long time, India…"

"You're going to see him again, right?" India asked, taking Kim's hands. "I mean, he sounds amazing and if he makes you feel this way… you should take a chance, you know? See what he's all about…"

"He's supposed to meet me for coffee tomorrow," Kim admitted, the both of them squealing and laughing with joy. It had been so long since either of them had gotten like this over a guy.

"Oh, that's so exciting, Kim." India nodded, embracing her

friend. "You deserve a good man and mountain man sounds like the real deal."

"His name is Malik, and he is amazing," Kim admitted, feeling giddy and lightheaded, remembering how she felt being alone with him. "I cannot wait to see him. I hope he shows up… I don't know how to get a hold of him if he doesn't. I don't think he has a cell phone."

"He'll show up," she assured, chuckling. "He'd be a total idiot if he didn't show up. You're an amazing and beautiful woman. If he doesn't show up, that's his loss."

"You're right." Kim smiled, embracing her. "But for now, which movie are we watching? The Photograph? Or Think Like a Man?"

"Both!" India insisted, winking at her friend. "We also have to figure out what you're going to wear tomorrow. You don't want it to be too casual…"

"We're going to need more tea…"

CHAPTER SEVEN

$\mathcal{M}$alik was standing in front of a small mirror he had hung up in the kitchen, checking his hair one final time. He had decided to wash it and trim it. He also shaved off the stubble of his beard and neck, unsure how he liked his bare face. He'd had a beard ever since he was old enough to grow one. It could have been because his own grandaddy's beard was long and untamed up until the day he died.

Looking at himself in the mirror, Malik considered the situation. He was dressed in his best blue jeans, boots, and button-up, one of the only non-plaid shirts he owned. It was a simple forest green shirt he'd purchased years ago in college and rarely wore, the sleeves and chest a bit tighter than he remembered. The shirt felt suffocating around his neck and arms, so he rolled the sleeves, stretching them around his forearms, and unbuttoned the first three buttons at his collar. This revealed the homemade pendant he wore, a gift from his grandfather on their last Christmas together made of shaped yellow-green Beryl surrounded by two light gray granite beads. It was all held together by thin leather strips and a single set of steel links that bound it around his neck.

His skin felt too tight and he was aware of his heartrate, slightly faster than normal. Was this normal? He was becoming alert as if he were hunting the passes for some sort of predator. It was an uncomfortable feeling, the cabin around him seeming to shrink as he threw on his simple brown Carhart jacket. Shutting the cabin door, he made for the barn, thoughts of the day's plans seeming to intensify this uneasy awareness. He was to meet Kim at the coffeeshop, a place he'd never been to in a town that probably wasn't aware he existed. However, the allure of seeing and speaking to Kim again outweighed this new nervousness.

He placed the saddle on Hen's back, offering her an apple from his jacket pocket as he clasped the straps and secured the reins. It wasn't long until he was leading her out of the barn to check on his two hens in their comfortably cozy coop. They were roosting quietly as he mounted Hen and urged her down the path toward the main trail. His mind wandered in the gray, green, and golden glow of the forest, Hen knowing her way to the ranger station without much direction from Malik.

Malik was focusing on his surroundings, but his mind was entirely consumed with Kim. She wasn't like other people he'd met, judging him for his distant upbringing or lack of social experience. She didn't treat him like a freak, something to be observed or fixed. That was his experience in college, only getting through because his professors and upperclassmen would encourage him to socialize and endure. That was something he never wanted to experience again. Those people and that place was far too restrictive, a system he just couldn't conform to.

As they reached the main road that led to the visitor center and ranger station, Malik spurred Hen forward into a trot and then a gallop, eventually reaching the slowly declining stretch of well-maintained trail where Hen could really stretch her legs. He sat low, urging her on down the trail as the breeze cooled his cheeks and neck, the scent of pine overwhelming as they came further down the mountain. It was twenty minutes later, after rounding the last descent that the well-kept lawns of the museum, visitor center, and ranger station came into view.

Sweetgum Lake was to the left, beyond the well-kept lawns of the Nature Center and Water Museum, the ranger station a large log cabin with a huge antenna atop it. Beyond was the parking lot and the main road that led south, into town. His heart pounded loudly as he approached the cabin, dismounting as his boss, and the head ranger, Lyle, came out onto the wrap-around porch.

"So, a date?" Lyle asked, a smile forming in his peppered beard. The word 'date' had Malik's heart skipping a beat.

"Just coffee, I should be back in an hour, maybe two," Malik explained a bit too frantically.

"When you supposed to meet the girl?" he asked, moving to sit on one of the rocking chairs as Hen grazed in the grass around the post.

"She said nine…"

"Then get going, keys are in it." Lyle nodded, pointing at the old Jeep with muddy tires and slight rust stains. "She's like a daughter to me, so be gentle."

"I haven't forgotten how to drive," Malik replied, grinning at Lyle's smirking expression.

"I was talking about the girl, boy," he warned, pointing a finger. "She's a local girl whose granny and I go way back. Be a gentleman or you'll have to answer to me."

"Understood," Malik affirmed, finding Lyle's warning to be just the tonic he needed to overcome the nervousness that filled him on his ride down the mountain. He was just going to meet her, have coffee, and extend the hand of friendship – there was nothing to be nervous about. If she rejected him, she'd be no different than countless strangers he'd met since he left that mountain in New Hampshire.

The drive south, less than a mile until the township limits, was dotted with the highlights of Sweetgum Meadows. Most just called it Sweetgum and the town had a sort of revitalization the past few years, housing developments attracting families and young people. Main Street, which he was heading south on, led slowly past Rochelle's Old-Fashioned Diner, Justin Time's Clock and Watch Repair, Sweet and Spicy Chinese Palace, and a business office for tax prep and lawyer services. It was here that he realized he needed to park, finding an open spot with a three-hour limit in front of the office. He had tried to pay attention to the other side of the road, a stretch of similar brick buildings stretching north and south along Main.

Roasted Beans Coffee Spot was across from the offices, a cozy set of big bay windows with a creative display and a daily menu enticing customers inside. It looked lively, sitting between the Scoop! There It Is! Ice Cream and Candy Shop and a small giftshop. Malik approached, looking at the bank clock that sat on the other side of the giftshop. He still had ten minutes and wondered if Kim was already there. He didn't see her on the street, an older couple leaving the bank and a group of women emerging from the daycare north across from the diner.

Malik squared his shoulders, opened the door to the coffee shop, and was immediately hit by the smell of roasting coffee and pastries. He didn't realize it would be busy, the main lounge area taken up by a few women who watched him as he came inside. The counter was empty, a woman standing behind it with a wide smile and a wave. She was friendly, young, and had her hair tied up under a bandana, her apron pinned with a nametag that read "Joanne."

"You look new here." She smiled, welcoming him up to the counter. "Am I right? You've never been here before?"

"Correct, first time here but I've lived around here for five years," Malik explained, seeing her curiosity and shock transform into excitement.

"Then, allow me to layout our shops daily specials and signature drinks." She nodded, pointing at the blackboard hanging above them. It had fanciful designs and great handwriting, Malik following along with Joanne as she explained the two main boards.

"This is our daily special board." Joanne smiled, pointing at one. "And today's special happens to be a sea-salt caramel mocha latte, made with our signature dark roast and almond milk. For an extra dollar you can choose any muffin or scone you'd like." She pointed to the other board. "This board is of our signature drinks; blends that we make year-round that have made my small franchise very popular in this area," she affirmed, pointing at a long list of mocha, latte, cappuccino, and Frappuccino concoctions. After spending a couple minutes listening to her, he smiled, remaining patient and polite.

"I'll just have a black coffee, house blend," he explained, pointing at the simplest thing on the menu. He was reluctant to admit he had no idea what most of the items on the menu were.

"I knew it," came a laugh from behind him, the door twinkling as Kim came in. The sight of her had a warm feeling settling over Malik. "Hi Joanne! Do you mind if we take the window?"

"Not at all, hun." Joanne smiled, waving at her. "The usual?"

"Please, the signature tea and a scone," she encouraged, smiling up at Malik. "I should have known you wouldn't be a whipped mocha with sprinkles kind of guy."

"How'd you guess?" he asked, smiling widely. He was relieved and surprisingly enthusiastic to see her, watching as she pushed her braids over her shoulder.

"Come, let's get comfortable." Kim smiled, leaving a five on the counter for Joanne. Malik pulled out his own wallet, realizing he only had twenties from his last ATM withdrawal over a month ago.

"I've got it." Kim smiled, winking at him as they moved around a few tables toward the large bay window. There was a sunken area near it, where a display used to be but instead there sat a coffee table surrounded by two armchairs and a loveseat. Surprisingly, she sat on the loveseat, staring up at him expectantly as she set her purse on the table.

"How's the rest of your week been?" he asked, sitting down next to her on the couch, sliding out of his jacket. He laid it over the arm of the couch and was surprised that she had done the same, removing her light jean jacket to reveal her soft blue blouse dotted with white and yellow flowers.

"It was good," she admitted, leaning back against the cushions. "I had a girl whose Sweet Sixteen was coming up soon, so she needed the perfect braids. I have to admit, even I was impressed with my own work."

The soft giggle and blush she let out only made Malik smile, his hands in his lap as Joanne came around Kim's shoulder with their order. She smiled kindly at Malik, squeezing Kim's shoulder before disappearing to tend to the new customers that had just walked in.

"Having pride in your work is always a good thing." Malik nodded, adding one packet of sugar from the coffee table to the coffee and stirring. "That's probably why I became a ranger."

"You're definitely brave but you make it seem so effortless." Kim chuckled, sipping her tea. She then cut up some of the scone, taking a bite with the small fork before grabbing a napkin. "You'll have to teach me how you became so confident."

"Me? Confident?" he asked, smirking at her. He was curious about how she viewed him. Did she really think he was brave? All he did was live in the woods, away from town. "Not in situations like this, in places like this. I'm a duck out of water…"

"You don't seem it," she said with a smile, sipping her tea. "Or are you putting on an act?"

"Social situations, with new people and places, make me nervous," he admitted, taking a drink of his coffee. "I guess you could say it's an act, but I only seem at ease because you're here."

"Oh?" she asked, blushing brightly. He hadn't really heard what he said until that moment, his own blush creeping up on his neck and ears as he tried to backtrack a little.

"W-well, I mean, I'm not used to social situations and you're the only reason I came into town today…" He wasn't sure what else to say, taking another drink of his coffee and staring out the window at the small-town traffic. That nervousness was creeping back into his belly, and he wasn't sure how to react.

"I understand, and I appreciate you coming into town," she assured, placing a hand on his arm, squeezing gently. She then ate some more of her scone, enjoying the soft café music and the chatter of the patrons. The silence between them was a bit awkward but Malik could feel the eyes on him in that moment. He didn't realize that he'd been watched by the regulars and Joanne ever since he wandered in. Did they know he wasn't one of them? Was he wearing the wrong thing? He adjusted the collar of his shirt and took another drink of his coffee

"I admit, I would have come to see you," Kim finally spoke, finishing her scone. "But I don't think I can remember the way, especially without the snow."

"It can be dangerous for inexperienced hikers," Malik admitted, grimacing. "But remember our bargain. I can teach you some survival basics if you want to learn."

"I would appreciate that, actually," Kim said with a nod, encouraging him to explain.

"Yeah, at the very least you should know how to find water, start a fire, find or make shelter, and I could probably show you what plants are safe to eat and use," he surmised, watching her face light up with curiosity. "I… enjoy rock climbing too."

"Really? You're so brave," she said with a nod, setting her cup down. "Could I ask you to teach me about that as well?"

"You seem eager." Malik chuckled, rubbing the back of his neck. "A fellow nature lover?"

"In my own ways." She shrugged, a twinkle in her eye. "But I want to learn and avoid being a burden out there."

"The wilderness isn't for everyone," Malik assured, hoping to ease her insecurities. "You don't have go back out there if you don't want to. Most people don't adapt well."

"I want to learn because I want to understand your life, your hobbies, better," she said, quite stubbornly. "Do you think I can do it?"

"I guess you won't know or learn if you don't try, right?"

"I like that approach." Kim nodded, moving closer, making Malik's heart skip a beat. "Are you available this weekend? I could come out and meet you at the park."

"We're expecting another storm Sunday, according to the National Weather Service," Malik warned, smiling over at her. "So, Saturday would be best."

"Saturday it is," she said as she smiled, her cheeks blushing cutely, making Malik smile down at her. "I'll find some hiking boots and buy a backpack."

"A walking stick is easy to find once you're on the trail," he replied, his voice low as he moved a little closer to her. "Bring a water canteen, first aid kit, and some matches too."

"Yes, sir," she replied, wrinkling her brow seriously. This made them both laugh, and the entire coffee shop seemed to notice the atmosphere they'd created together.

CHAPTER EIGHT

So far, Kim's morning date with Malik had gone exceptionally well though part of her questioned if it really was a date. Kim knew it was a date, they had connected, but she was just surprised she'd landed one with someone so amazing. Every word spoken from Malik's perfect lips wrapped Kim in his soothing, deep voice. He was fascinating and warm, despite living an isolated life she knew nothing about. That didn't matter because he was able to intrigue and enchant her with the passion he had for that life.

Kim didn't want to interrupt Malik, didn't want to leave this warm glow between them, but she desperately needed to use the bathroom. The tea always had this effect, but she loved it so much.

"I really need to use the bathroom. Don't go anywhere." Kim smirked, waiting for a pause to speak up. "I want to hear more when I get back."

Malik's dark eyes met with Kim's as he laughed deeply. "I'll be right here."

Kim stood up and walked carefully to the bathroom in the back. She didn't want to make a mad dash for the door, running into someone or appearing like she was frantic. Kim managed to be quick inside, washing her hands, and stepping out of the small, dimly lit room with a spritz of perfume from her purse. She decided to pace herself on the way back to Malik, noticing the looks he was getting. He was sitting facing away from her at the window, sipping on his now empty cup of coffee. Even the back of his head was alluring, making her blush at the heads he was turning.

Glancing around, Kim realized she was not the only one ogling Malik. A few women were sneaking glances at him, and as a woman entered the coffee shop, she did a double take, clearly checking Malik out. Kim wasn't jealous of these rubbernecking women; in fact, she didn't mind. Malik was a very handsome man and was new to everyone in town, including the single women.

A hand reached for Kim's arm and gently pulled her aside, stepping into the small office and storage near the bathroom. Joanne, the owner, giggled with a hand over her face.

"Who is that fine slice of man and where have you been hiding him?" Joanne asked, pointing around the corner at Malik. Kim looked abashed and shook her head, amused by Joanne's question. She should have known Joanne would stop her to chat about her newly found stranger.

"He's a park ranger and I wasn't hiding him, I promise." Kim chuckled, her voice low as they both stared at him from that back hallway. At this rate, Kim may have to hide him because it seemed like every woman was thinking about a fine slice of Malik.

"I'm so thrilled to see you found a wonderful man to call your own," Joanne sighed, clasping her hands together and shaking them slightly. There was an overly excited glisten in her bright hazel eyes.

"Malik and I just met each other. It isn't anything serious

yet." Kim smiled, watching from around the corner to see if Malik was searching for her yet.

"Oh, I like that word… yet." Joanne smirked, raising an eyebrow as though disappointed in Kim. "I see the way that man looks at you. He's been flirting and chatting with you for almost an hour. It might not be serious yet, but that man has already fallen."

Kim chuckled and waved to Joanne, passing off her comment with a kind smile and a wink. Did Malik truly have feelings for her? Is that what it looked like to everyone else? The thought sent butterflies to her stomach. However, the closer she approached and the more she thought about it, the giddy feeling turned toward fear. She was scared to dive right in with someone she just met, but she felt so comfortable with him, so unlike the so-called date she had that led to meeting him. He was kind and courteous, handsome, and wholesome and she just needed to know more. Back at the window, Kim sat down next to Malik who perked up at her sudden return.

"Sorry I took so long," she said, pushing her braids over her blue blouse's shoulder. Kim wanted to tell him what Joanne said, wanted to gauge his reaction, but didn't want to embarrass him.

"That's okay." Malik's smile was intoxicating.

Kim caught a few women that lived in town but were out of place at the coffee shop. They stopped by to basically gawk at Malik twenty minutes ago, chatting with Joanne when they arrived. Kim rolled her eyes, moving a little closer to Malik. She wanted to shrug them off the best she could, but she suddenly felt extremely jealous and insecure. She may have to get used to all the unwanted attention, but Malik didn't seem to take notice of the women. Kim had noticed it the moment she walked in, which made the pride in her chest swell. He kept his eyes only on Kim that entire time they sat in the coffee shop.

"How much time do you have before work?" he asked,

finishing his second coffee. He set his cup down on the coffee table, his tone telling Kim he had something in mind if she had the time.

Kim waved her hand in a circle. "Oh, my first client isn't until one. I don't have any appointments until later this afternoon."

"I'd really love to spend more time with you, if that's okay."

"What if I showed you around town?" she asked, a bit breathless. She wasn't sure if he had plans for the morning, but she figured it was a good idea to show him around. He never spent much time away from his cabin and he seemed to have acclimated to the coffeeshop.

"I'd love that." Malik nodded. Before they left, he went and broke a twenty-dollar bill with Joanne and left a five on the counter.

As they walked out together, Malik offered to hold open her jacket for her and opened the jangling front door.

"Lead the way," Malik gestured, holding open the glass door. As she passed him, she could smell the forest he lived in on his clothes. It was woodsy and warm like she was back at his cabin already.

Outside the coffee shop, Kim decided to keep on Main Street, heading north on that same side of the road. An idea had popped into her head, that she wasn't sure if Malik would appreciate but it was something she could reveal about herself to him.

"I'd love to show you the comic store. They have video games, board games, and all sorts of stuff," Kim suggested, walking north past the candy and ice cream shop. "It's the next shop down."

"No, I, uhm, don't play video games, but I'll go wherever you want to go," he admitted, blushing slightly. "I'm more into puzzles, card games, and woodworking."

Kim chuckled at having even asked if the outdoorsy man like

video games. She couldn't imagine him up there playing Nintendo in his cabin. "I love going there for manga."

Malik tilted his head quizzically at her. "What's manga?"

Kim attempted to think of a simple way to explain it to Malik, unsure if the subtle difference between manga, comics, and graphic novels really mattered to him.

"Uhm, like books with lots of pictures like in comics." She smiled, glancing at the people who stared as they walked by. "But instead of starting at the front of the book, you start at the end. The art style is very different than regular comic books too, as they originate in Japan."

She could see Malik trying to figure it out, his mind working behind those dark alluring eyes. Kim felt like she put him out of his comfort zone after a moment, stopping just outside the shop. "We could go somewhere else though. I don't mind."

Malik shook his head. "No, I want to check out this manga with you. I'd love to learn about what you're interested in."

Kim's smile spread and it was painfully obvious she was excited to share her world with him. She led Malik into the store, practically skipping with each step. She felt Malik's eyes on her even as others passing them stared at him. He was so fixated, and Kim loved every second of it.

The bell above Nerd Central Comics and Video Game Store's door dinged when Kim pulled it open.

"Hey," came the sullen voice of the owner, Demetrius. It sounded almost like a grunt, then he stuck his nose back in the comic he was reading at the counter. Kim caught a glance at the cover seeing it was one of the Spider Man comics.

Kim leaned her head close to Malik and whispered, "That's Demetrius. He's the local grumpy guy." She chuckled.

On the far wall, Kim picked out the next book in one of her most favorite series. It was the latest volume, and she was ecstatic that it was finally in stock. She then showed him the style of several different popular titles before moving to popular comics and graphic novels. She showed him different styles and storylines, but he seemed content to hear her talk.

Malik trailed after Kim as she walked her manga volume to the counter and set it down gently. Demetrius peered up from his comic and sat it facedown, still open to keep his place. He scanned the book and the price popped up in bright green on the screen attached to the register.

Malik moved himself next to Kim at the counter and pulled out his wallet. "Can I get that for you?" He looked to Kim for approval. Hesitant at first, Kim nodded and allowed Malik to buy the book for her.

"Thank you, so much."

Book in hand, with a smile at Demetrius, Kim followed Malik toward the door. Before they could leave, Demetrius grumbled behind them, his voice full of more life than Kim had heard in a long while.

"You be good to her, you hear me, kid? She's too nice a lady to mess with layabouts."

Malik chuckled, making Kim blush furiously. She could feel his eyes on her, but she was focused on Demetrius, who watched Malik sternly.

"I promise you, sir, I'm no layabout."

Outside the store, Kim and Malik casually made their way north to the crosswalk. She felt a bit awkward after that, the pressure starting to make her aware of almost everything she did. It was torture almost, unable to decide how she wanted Malik to see the real her.

"Want to go to the diner? Get a proper brunch?"

"Brunch? Ah, breakfast and lunch," he said as he smiled, chuckling, and making her knees weak. "Clever." Malik's approval was all she wanted, hoping to spend as much time with him as possible that day. The thought that she might not see him until the weekend was becoming painful.

Maybe it was about time Kim talked to Rochelle. She hadn't

seen the matchmaking diner owner since the date she had set up for her earlier that week. Inside the diner, Kim was able to locate Rochelle instantly as she was chatting with customers. Rochelle had grown wide-eyed and held her arms out towards Kim for a hug when she spotted her.

"I've heard a lot about what happened on your date," Rochelle whispered, glancing at Malik. "So, I have to ask, are you okay, hun? I'm so sorry he wasn't what I thought he was…"

"Pick a table, please." Kim smiled, squeezing Malik's jacket sleeve. "I'll be back in a minute with drinks."

He nodded, smiling kindly at Rochelle before picking a booth near the window and small stage. The two women watched him as he slipped off his jacket again, revealing the strain of his shirt around his biceps and chest. Rochelle was almost drooling, and Kim couldn't help but enjoy the view as well. They then disappeared into the kitchen, the waitresses instantly noticing Malik.

Kim spilled every detail of her horrendous date and cold, stormy night once they got into the office, just as she had with India. Rochelle cringed, horrified at the story and her role in it.

"I'm so sorry. I never would have set you up with that man if I'd known he would do that to you."

The question that had been on Kim's mind for a while just slipped out. "But how well do you know him?"

Rochelle shifted on her feet and covered her mouth for a split second, then confessed what Kim had hoped was not the case.

"I only met him a handful of times when he came into the diner. I'm so embarrassed and I feel awful." She shifted her attention to Malik, glancing at him from the window of the kitchen. "Thank God he was there to help you. I can't believe that little son of a—" Rochelle paused to avoid cussing. "He deserves a good wallop if he shows his face in here again."

Malik smiled at the waitress, who tried to flirt and take his order. Kim quickly grabbed some glasses and a pitcher of iced Georgia sweet tea. Kim wanted to make sure Rochelle wouldn't get too worked up and explained the situation.

"Please don't worry about that idiot. Besides, it all worked out okay in the end," Kim spoke, striding from the kitchen as Malik noticed her watching him. She looked into Malik's eyes and something unspoken passed between them and electricity that even Rochelle admired from a distance.

CHAPTER NINE

*P*arting from Kim was a bit uneasy, Malik wanting to walk her to work; however, she insisted she could walk there alone. He said goodbye to her and reconfirmed their meetup for that Saturday at the park, making sure she knew to check in at the ranger station. She agreed and after a slow, awkward, and slightly clumsy goodbye, he offered his hand, seeing her appreciation for the small but intimate gesture.

After reaching the Jeep, he decided to take a loop around town, seeing the main street fully before heading south to the town square and park where most of the holiday and historical events took place. He saw there was a convention hall and a grocery store heading west out of town near the fields and pastures of the fruit plantations. To the east, past the park, gazebo, and staging grounds was nothing but housing developments. It was only coming back north, toward the Sweetgum Park and Trails that other, traditional streets of small houses, emerged to the east, residential streets lined with family homes.

He wove up and down these streets, spotting the schools, hospital, and library before slowing down in front of the historic Sweetgum Meadows Baptist Church. It had a plaque outside it, with bronze letters declaring it to be over 150 years old and a dedicated heritage site for the county. It was a quaint but busy town, and Malik wondered why he had never ventured through it so thoroughly before now.

After turning from the church and driving past the elementary school where children yelled at recess, he turned north again on Main Street, eager to get back to Hen and their familiar mountain home. Pulling into the park, he noticed there were a few more hikers than normal, the Nature Center and Water Museum buzzing with activity. He also saw a few people standing near the ranger station, talking to Lyle and the other two local rangers – Emry and Levi.

"There he is," Lyle spoke from his rocking chair, Hen tied comfortably to the tree where she stood grazing happily. "We were wondering when you'd be back, Malik."

"Yeah, these ladies were just asking about our ranger program." Emry smirked, making one of the women blush.

"How about you ladies come back for the museum's weekly nature display and lecture?" Levi suggested, winking at another woman. "It's every Thursday and then I do believe the Sweetgum Museum Partners meet next week to discuss their annual fundraiser and conservation drive."

"You ladies want to save the planet?" Emry asked, taking a serious tone.

"Of course." They nodded, turning from the smirking young men toward the museum and nature center.

"What was that about?" Malik asked, eyes wide as he stepped up onto the porch to sit next to Lyle. "Lots of visitors today, huh?"

"Thanks to a certain someone's efforts with his new lady friend," Lyle explained, making Emry and Levi chuckle. "That's the third group of women who have come here asking about rangers and our conservation efforts."

"I asked them what spurred their interest, and they said a

particularly handsome ranger and his girlfriend," Levi teased, nudging Emry. "But I can see why they were so fascinated… you been walking around with your biceps and pecs hanging out all morning!"

"It's the nicest shirt I own," Malik shot back, crossing his arms. "And it wasn't even that cold today."

"But you rescued your damsel, yeah?" Levi asked, crossing his arms as well. "You going to be the sexy knight in shining armor that swept her off her feet, Romeo?"

"She isn't a damsel." Malik shrugged, making them all pause. "She's a woman, and despite not being familiar with survival techniques or the area, I have a feeling she would have made it out all right even if I hadn't found her. She's just like that…"

"He's a hermit," Emry scoffed, eyeing the women standing outside the museum. "And he's attracting these fine honeys right to our doorstep. As far as I'm concerned, he can rescue as many damsels as he wants, so long as I get to enjoy these kinds of perks."

"You two are animals; no wonder why you ain't got no women." Lyle shrugged, smirking at Malik. "At least this one has some respect."

"And common sense." Malik shrugged, standing again. "But Hen and I are going to get back so I can get some stuff done. You still need me to mark those trees?"

"I think surveyors and the logging company commissioned by the state will be in next week, so take your time," Lyle said with a nod, standing from his chair as well. "Just make sure to mark the dying and keep track of the diseased ones."

"Can do, boss." Malik nodded in agreement, stepping down from the porch and walking toward Hen.

It wasn't long until the pair were back on the trail north, winding away from the lake, kept grasses, and quaint cabin-feel of the ranger station and museum. The greenery around him was bright and warm as his mind contemplated the events of that morning. He had been so content in Kim's company, that even now, in the familiar stretches of forest and mountain, he felt uneasy. Something was wrong and as his mind mulled it, his ears picked up on some odd noises ahead.

Off the trail, atop a knoll surrounded by bramble and smaller pines, was a huge pine, towering over all the rest of the trees. The very top branches were bright, deep green and browning at the tips, but below most of the branches were amber and empty. This tree was definitely meant to be marked for the loggers but standing around it, and climbing in it, were a group of twenty-somethings foolishly taking pictures with their selfie sticks and phones.

"Hey!" Malik called out, making all four of them freeze. "That's dangerous, please come down before you get hurt."

The two men in the tree complied, nodding as they were able to shimmy to the ground safely and join their female friends. They all looked slightly ashamed and weren't expecting a man on a horse to come galloping up to them and start yelling.

"Sorry to have startled you but I'm a park ranger and that tree is ancient and fragile," he explained, keeping his voice calm and light. "Did you not see the excess of dead pine needles and fallen cones? The bare branches? The oozing sap on the bark of the trunk? This tree is on its last limb and has to be felled."

"Sorry, we just wanted some great shots for social media, raising awareness and everything," one of the men spoke up, showing him the video. "We weren't doing anything."

"If you are raising awareness for social media, you should have known better than to be climbing on a tree like that," Malik said, a bit more tersely than he would have liked. Hen swayed and nickered, nipping at the ground around her.

"How are we supposed to know what kind of tree it is, or not to climb on it?" one of the women shot back, hands on her hips.

Anger was pressing at Malik's chest, but she was right. As far as he knew, public schools didn't teach common guidelines to follow in national parks. There was plenty on the local national park websites, but one would have to go looking for it to find it. The thought didn't entirely quench his anger though.

"It's commonly called a Georgia pine and it looks to be over two hundred years old. It could fall at any time, and you could have injured yourselves or others."

"We didn't mean to," one of the men said, coming down to the path.

"I wonder why it's dying," one of the others said, quietly looking up at it. She pointed her cell at it and took a few more shots.

"It could be various reasons," Malik explained, pointing at the canopy of the forest. "Trees are a lot like the connections of nerves in the body. Their roots and tops are intermingled, making their own respective ecosystems. Throwing any of it off, even just a little bit, can destroy hundreds of years of growth and history."

"We had no idea," the younger dark-haired woman admitted. "That's so sad."

"Just be careful to not do it again," Malik said, hoping they would remember his lesson. Hen was still munching, swaying as Malik held her in place. "And make sure you read over the guidelines on the national park website before coming back out again. I think it's a good time to exit the park for the day now."

They mumbled half-hearted apologies, and he swore one of the men rolled his eyes at the other. How could they be so careless while claiming to be trying to raise awareness? Was pretending to care some sort of fad he didn't know about? It brought back the point that the woman had raised. How were they supposed to have known about basic rules such as not climbing a dying tree—or even knowing what one looks like—if they didn't know the rules existed?

He took off up the trail toward the main rise of the mountain cliffs while still processing both their carelessness and the lack of public knowledge about the wilderness. He and Hen had come to their usual spot where the main trail had several converging trails springing from it. Like a river cutting through a valley, the trails wound and interwove and lead them onward, up to the weaving vertical trail.

Malik's mind wandered as they made their final ascent, ready to get back to the cabin and do his chores as well as prepare for Kim's arrival that upcoming weekend. Nervousness began to wash over him again and he couldn't help but distract himself with anger for the careless hikers and social media addicts. Their carelessness, and inconsiderate actions were not an isolated incident. Most people just didn't understand, or care to understand, just how fragile the wilderness is. They couldn't possibly understand if they didn't care, and they didn't care because they avoid it like a plague.

Perhaps it just wasn't his problem but when they approached the cabin and stable, Malik couldn't help but wonder how people could be better informed. It was clear that he couldn't be there to educate every group, but he could give some pointers that might help out the nature center and ranger station. He pondered this a bit longer as he got Hen settled and his own cabin lit up with candles and a fire. Something was still bugging him as he ate his dinner, some canned vegetables and stew stored in the root cellar beneath the floorboards. Something ate at him, and it might have been his unease over Kim and their date but there was more to it than that. The idea of it being a date hadn't even crossed his mind until that moment, which derailed him even further from thoughts of informing ignorant, selfie-seeking hikers.

CHAPTER TEN

Kim was disappointed to part ways with Malik, but it was time to head into work. She walked to the salon wishing for more time in the day. On the other hand, she was in high spirits that their first date had gone so well. She clutched the book in her hand, excited to begin reading it. Maybe she would start it that night curled on the couch with a snuggly warm blanket.

Inside the salon, Kim greeted her co-workers with a delighted smile. She got right to setting up her workstation, and just as she finished, her first client of the day strolled in. Kim began working on her and chatting about what was new and how she was doing.

Jessica barged out of the wash area, startling a customer. "Whose turn was it to clean the shampoo sinks yesterday?" Kim narrowed her eyes at Jessica. No matter what the issue was, she had no right to disrupt customers.

"It was my turn, and I did it," Kim explained, a pleasant smile still plastered on her face. Kim swore Jessica sensed when she was having a good day because she'd been able to find the smallest ways to ruin them for a long time.

Jessica's outburst and loud voice caught their boss' attention though, Jessica making sure she noticed. She batted her eye lashes, playing innocent, and scowled at Kim. "Did you? They're so caked with grime I couldn't tell." Jessica turned away, striding off with her perfect hair bouncing off her back in rhythm with her exaggerated steps.

Kim shook her head, fuming inside. She was becoming tired of Jessica's comments and lashing out. She just wanted to work on her client's hair but Kalie in the chair next to Kim leaned over and whispered kind of loud.

"What is going on between you two?"

Kim shrugged but wasn't even sure she knew the answer. It was like Jessica was looking for ways to disrupt Kim's work life. "I have no idea. She's been snipping at me these past few days and I don't even know what I did to her." Kim smiled, trying to keep it lighthearted. "Must be a bad day for her."

"Jessica can be prickly," Treena chimed in, ready to join the gossip. She sighed and looked at her own nails. "It's too bad Jessica is such a great manicurist, otherwise, boss woman would probably get rid of her."

Kim thought of the cute snowflake design Jessica had on her nails yesterday and agreed, enjoying some of her more creative designs.

"She does have talent when it comes to nails." Kim nodded, braiding one of her client's hair. Kim had always been great with hair, but she was terrible at doing nails. The designs always ended up smudged and wobbly to the point you could hardly recognize what it was meant to be. If Jessica were a little friendlier, Kim would have asked her to teach her how to do a basic French manicure. The white tips alone would be uneven whenever Kim tried.

Then Lilia smiled at Kim, her bright eyes lighting up. "Don't worry too much about Jessica. I saw those sinks and there was nothing wrong with them. She's making it up." She waved her hand in the air with a small flick of her wrist, smiling kindly at her customer.

A few other regulars passed through the salon that afternoon and Kim knocked out their appointments with ease. They were ecstatic to allow Kim to take pictures of their finished hair to post to her social media, which consumed the late afternoon as did deciding where they wanted to order food from. Kim had been trying to build a brand online for herself one picture at a time. Clients loved going on her page to see their hair as well. Kim had done well with the page's aesthetics and had over two thousand followers. She hoped one day she would be a world-recognized braid artist and hairdresser, but it took one step at a time.

Rochelle had come in for her typical appointment, apologizing again and again and taking a tongue lashing from her co-workers. Rochelle was so sorry she offered to comp their dinner, and all was settled over some delicious mocktails and sandwiches. Even Joanna stopped in after closing her coffee shop to chat and get her hair trimmed and washed. The girls had fun gossiping, Jessica mostly sticking to her clients, chatting with them, and shooting annoyed looks at the others when they started cackling like hens.

It didn't matter to Kim, the afternoon slowing so that she was able to post the pictures between customers. Kim finished during a longer lull between her appointments, posting a few creative braids on her page. The unique nature-themed and tribal motifs on her photos and posts was shared and retweeted more than a thousand times, making her smile as she cleaned up her station. It was not long before she noticed she had a DM. Kim didn't usually get messages on there, so curiosity gripped her. She checked the message and stopped stiffly with her broom in one hand and her phone in the other.

The message was from a very high-profile celebrity who lived in Atlanta. She wanted Kim to do her hair for an event and was willing to come all the way out to Sweetgum to get it done. Kim jumped to life, yelling excitedly as the rest of the stylists, and clients, watched her.

"Oh my God!" she yelled, turning her phone to show her nearest co-worker. The other salon workers stared at her puzzled, but her co-worker's face immediately lit up. She began jumping up and down, laughing, and congratulating Kim, which made them all even more puzzled. So, Kim rushed to each of them to show the message off. The older women didn't understand but her other co-workers were beyond ecstatic.

"She's been blowing up on social and Spotify!" Treena smiled.

"What are you waiting for? Message her back," Lilia urged, waving her hands in the air.

Kim realized she left the message on read. She quickly replied, explaining she'd love to work for them and that she had several appointments available the afternoon a day before the event and the morning of the event. Kim sent the message and stared at her phone for the reply. It came quicker than she thought it would. These people did not mess around. The woman secured an appointment for the afternoon the day before her event. Those few moments thrilled Kim as she finished up the conversation and tucked her phone away, elated and fluttering.

Treena, Kalie, and Lilia were all around Kim and had smiles stuck to their faces while the clients and older owner and stylists just smiled at their giddy excitement. They congratulated Kim and her boss surprised her with a large hug.

"I'm so proud of you, Kim. I always knew you were going places." Kalie grinned, nudging her. "A real celebrity, in my salon!"

Kim grinned as her boss dropped her arms. "Thank you." She glanced around the salon, beaming with happiness as the other girls talked about a deep clean and some updates to the decor.

Jessica caught Kim's eye then, the look absolutely unmistakable. She had been in the corner, glaring daggers at Kim the whole time. As their eyes met for a split second, Kim almost felt bad for her. She'd been waiting for her big break as well. Jessica narrowed her eyes further then spun on her heels and marched into the back room. The sense of discomfort, and pity, washed over her and she wondered what she could do to help mend this bridge.

CHAPTER ELEVEN

Saturday came around quicker than he had expected it to, Malik reaching the ranger station and park early for his day with Kim. He had ridden Hen back down the trails that morning, the mare eager to gallop and graze in the usually green grasses of the museum and nature center. She seemed in a particularly good mood that morning, Levi taking her off his hands as Lyle met him on the porch. Malik was almost a half hour early and wondered if he'd been a bit too casual with his outfit.

"Nervous?" Lyle asked, smirking up at him. "I remember that feeling, despite bein' a hundred years old."

"If you're a hundred, then I must be in my sixties." Malik laughed, sitting on the step of the porch. "But we're just going for a hike, and I'm going to try and teach her some basic survival tricks."

"Remember what I said last time," Lyle hummed, his warning before their first date at the coffee shop still echoing in Malik's mind. "I've known her since she was born."

"You've got nothing to worry about with me," Malik assured, watching the bright blue sky above. There were only a few wisps of white cloud and the sounds of geese at the ponds, preparing for their migration back north, signaled the ending of that record-breaking winter. It would soon be March and then spring would be bringing all the animals and bugs out of their winter slumber.

It was then that a small truck pulled into the park, the first of the day. Malik wasn't sure what vehicle he was watching for but when the third showed up, just a few minutes later, he spotted Kim's familiar smile and braided hair. She was in a small silver car, and when she stepped out, he could see she had taken his instruction seriously.

She was wearing a pair of jeans, a long t-shirt with some sort of Georgia Peach logo, and an old pair of boots. She grabbed a small backpack from her front seat, locking the car and stuffing the keys in her bag before approaching the ranger station. She looked excited, a bit nervous, but the determination and confidence in her stride only made Malik smile. She was an interesting woman, unlike any he'd met before, and he wondered if the intentionally tight and neat way she wove together her braids atop her head was for practical reasons. If so, Malik admired her adaptability and hoped Kim was a fast learner.

"Is that Miss Kim?" Lyle asked, standing, and emerging from the shade of the covered porch.

"Uncle Lyle!" she called out, waving enthusiastically. "How have you been? I haven't seen you since the New Year's Day Icicle Festival."

"Should have waited and had ourselves a snowman competition this week." Lyle chuckled, reaching out to hug her as he descended the stairs. "It's been a while. How's your granny? She still givin' yer momma grief?"

"What else would granny be doing?" Kim smiled, hugging him gently before turning to Malik. "I got what you asked. Water canteen, thirty-two ounces, with a first aid kit and two packs of matches. I also decided that a compass and a poncho might also be a smart bet along with an extra pair of socks."

"Remember what I taught y'all in school then?" Lyle chuckled, eyeing Malik knowingly. "Stay safe out there. Cams have picked up more deer and turkeys so watch out for predators."

"We'll be back before the day's end," Kim assured, patting Lyle's arm before turning to the trails leading into the woods and mountains. "Ready?"

"Are you?" Malik smiled, waving at Lyle.

"I am, and I've got some great news," she admitted, keeping pace with him as he grabbed his pack out of the saddle bag that sat astride the pasture fence.

"Tell me," he insisted, hoisting the pack on his back. He was curious about her good news and only hoped she would feel comfortable sharing it with him. Though they had only met a week ago, he wanted to know everything about Kim.

"I have an appointment with a celebrity client at the salon," Kim gushed, the blush and excited trill of her voice forcing a wide smile to spread across his face. "Since I'm building a brand online using social media, it is absolutely perfect for exposure and advertising. I'm so excited!"

"That's amazing, congratulations," Malik encouraged, motioning for her to follow him as they made their way up one of the easier uphill treks over Sweetgum Lake below. "I'm not on social media but if I were, I'd try to figure out how to add you as a friend." They both giggled at this, the happiness in her honey brown eyes only enchanting him further as the smell of pine and her vanilla perfume overwhelmed.

"Would you like to see my work?" she asked, pulling out her phone.

"Absolutely." He smiled, pausing under a tree so the glare wasn't so intense.

"I've been trying to show off my braids and styles as classic and time-honored but also new, sort of like a steam-punk feel but with more natural elements," she explained, showing him the photos on the small screen.

The various braids of all shapes and sizes were amazing, creating designs and patterns that accented the various accessories that Kim had included in each picture. He liked the photos in black and white with pops of color in the accessories and shading. It drew his eye and really made the dark intricate patterns of the many-sized braids stand out. He admired her creativity and her excitement as she told him about each client as if they were a friend of hers. The way she was friendly, kind, and able to light up the faces of her friends and clients fascinated Malik. She was someone he could never be, someone who understood social cues, small talk, and all the things that he had to figure out on his own.

It wasn't as if he was raised as an animal, but his grandfather never taught him how to interact, talk to, and read people, something Kim seemed very good at doing. After looking through her social posts, and her brand on social media, Malik was certain that this brilliantly excitable woman was the first person he'd ever considered a future with. It was a sudden, and frightening thought that made him take a step away, her eyes going up to meet his quizzically.

"Okay?" she asked, lowering her phone. "You look a little ill."

"I just realized that I don't know anything about social media or these new phone trends," he muttered, trying to distract himself from what he was feeling for Kim. "It's a little embarrassing but I don't even own a cell phone."

"That's different but not embarrassing." She smiled, squeezing his arm. "What is embarrassing is not knowing how to read a compass."

Malik laughed at this, the twinkle in her eyes only fueling on his determination to at least teach her something of value while they were there. He pulled out his own compass from the pack, showing it to her and explaining how it works. He wasn't a physicist, but he understood the basics and told her that no matter what, that needle will always point north.

As they were walking down the trail, with Kim in front to guide them using her newly learned skills, Malik spotted some telltale signs of deer as well as wild flocks of turkeys. She seemed even more fascinated as he pointed out the different tracks. There were also feathers spread across the forest floor as they reached a popular bluff for feeding birds. The berries that lined the bushes and trees here were a preferred grazing grounds for bugs and birds and in the spring, popular with butterflies.

"As you can see," Malik showed her, pointing at some turkey tracks and molted feathers, "They like to roost together, in a sort of cluster, for safety. They are pretty stupid creatures, but they take care a lot of pests like ticks, fleas, and mosquitos."

"Can you hunt turkeys?"

"Only certain times of year," he assured, pointing over the bluff at the lake and lodge below. "We allow hunters in to keep the population under control but rangers like myself are allowed to hunt for sustainable living."

"You'll have to teach me more about the animals out here on this mountain," she insisted, walking next to him as they made their way across the scenic bluff. "I'm a local girl so I know to avoid certain snakes and bugs, but I don't know much about the larger animals, like predators."

"Those are always the ones that people want to know about," he admitted, pointing at some signs of deer activity. "And the predators will be hunting more openly in the weeks to come. Winter is coming to an end."

"And if I were to encounter a predator, hiking, what should I do?" she asked, smirking up at him.

"The predators around here vary but large cats and bears are the worst of it," he explained, seeing her eyes light up with curiosity and attentive hunger. The rest of the day seemed to continue like this as they hiked around the bluffs and into the mountain passes where she had found herself abandoned last time. He showed her how to find the game paths, signs of water, what plants were poisonous, and the kinds of plants that were edible. Kim was paying close attention to his instruction and picked up on the small lessons quickly.

During their hike, Malik found out that Kim loved tea from around the world, made her passion for hair into her career, and wanted more than anything to help improve her hometown of Sweetgum Meadows. She told him she loved soul and jazz music, that both her parents were alive and still lived in Sweetgum, and that she had a best friend, who was like a sister, named India. She also told him that despite knowing everyone in town, she wasn't very social, envying his life of quiet seclusion close to nature.

"It's the quiet life that's constantly testing me," Malik admitted, finding a comfortable spot near a set of large stones for them to relax before descending back down the mountain towards the main visitor center. "To be honest, when my grandaddy died, I didn't think I'd have anyone else to enjoy nature with. I thought for sure I'd never feel comfortable around another person again so I'm glad you're here."

"Well, I'm glad you feel comfortable with me." Kim smiled, sitting down next to him as they looked across the woods and hills that led down to the lake. "I feel really comfortable with you too. Usually, I just have my own small group of friends that I've known for years but with you, Malik, it feels different."

His name on her lips sounded amazing and he wanted to hear it again, smiling serenely at her as she spoke about the town and her friends. He learned about Rochelle the matchmaking owner of the diner and her chef and close friend Nick. Kim also spoke about Joanne and then her eyes lit up at the mention of a book club.

"The people in Sweetgum Meadows are really welcoming and kind," Kim explained, squeezing his arm excitedly. "You should come with me to book club Monday night!"

"Oh, a book club?" Malik asked, basking in the glow of her enthusiasm.

"You don't have to read the book if you don't want," she assured, nudging him playfully. "It's mostly a chance for everyone to get together and eat. We hold the meetings at Rochelle's diner after hours and everyone brings a dish, sort of potluck style."

"It sounds interesting," he admitted, still feeling wary of jumping right into the community. Kim was an insider, a local, and used to the people in town. Malik didn't want to be the subject of judgement or ridicule. However, the expectant wide honey eyes of Kim immediately made that nervousness disappear. The idea of spending more time with her so soon was worth any sort of social situation – she was worth the effort.

"All right, I think I can make it," he agreed, nudging her playfully as she squeezed his arm. "I'll meet you at the diner and bring my venison chili."

"Oh, that was so delicious," she said with a smile, springing up from next to him on the set of rocks and boulders. "I can't wait to introduce you to some of the members."

"Well, I think we should head back down the mountain since its almost noon," Malik proposed, looking at his watch. "But before we go, how about you learn the ultimate skill? A skill learned and perfected by man a long-long time ago."

"I can do it, teach me," she urged, stepping toward him with confidence.

"All right, you're going to learn how to gather for, build, and light a fire." Malik winked, making her blush brightly.

It didn't take long to show her the difference between dry and wet branches, brush, and wind patterns before setting up the small but well-ventilated fire. He then demonstrated, with some rocks and a dry stick how to light the fire properly. Though she had matches, he wanted her to see how she could build a fire, even in windy or wet conditions. It only took her a couple tries on her own, but she was finally able to get it, jumping up with an excited scream.

"I did it!" She smiled, springing to her feet and dancing about. "I can't believe it!"

"Keep feeding it," Malik instructed, pointing at the small pile of dry leaves, needles, and small sticks. "It'll grow and stay lit but pay attention to the wind and embers."

She giggled and squealed with excitement, kneeling down to build up the fire before leaning back against the rocks to watch it. Malik nodded his approval, enjoying the crackle and scent of burning pine. The flicker of golden light dashed around them, and they relax a bit longer, talking quietly about the book club's fiction selection. In the flickering glow of the fire, Kim looked absolutely adorable, her excitement and enthusiasm reflected in the enchanting twinkle of her eyes. Those beautiful, round, and hypnotizing eyes that wouldn't let him drop his gaze.

She noticed he was staring at her intently and she smiled up at him, his heart melting instantly. It was a beautiful smile, with a dimple in one cheek, and a small birthmark above her brow moving as their stare intensified. Her brow was furrowed but then relaxed, staring up at him intently as he leaned forward slowly. He didn't want to scare Kim, or pressure her, but she didn't pull away, watching him as their lips came together tentatively.

It was a soft breath, like the touch of a feather, but then it intensified, their eyes closing as their hands found one another. Kim's fingers grasped gently at the front of his shirt while his own arms wrapped around her hips lightly. They were melding together, close and intimate as their lips battled one another passionately. Malik didn't want it to end but soon they had pulled apart, slightly breathless, with the crackle of the flames adding to the atmosphere that felt so comfortable between them.

CHAPTER TWELVE

*K*im hustled up Main Street, staring into the windows of all the small family-owned stores as she passed them. The cool air made her pull her jacket tighter, but the sun's warmth kissed her cheeks. Her walk didn't last long as she arrived in front of Rochelle's Diner, opening the door with the jingle of the bell and entering the heated building. She immediately sighed in relief, taking a deep breath, getting a whiff of a mixture of delicious smelling foods.

There, in the front, sat the variety of members in the book club. They took up the entire diner, chatting and mingling. The hum of conversation felt like a hug and a few people waved in her direction. Behind them was set up a row of tables along the wall with an assortment of food set out for the potluck style meal that evening. Kim had brought her favorite pecan pie recipe from her grandma, usually a highlight of the dessert table.

Tugging off her jacket, she hung it on the coatrack by the door. Excitement for the event grew as Kim was greeted by smiling faces and welcoming hellos from people she mingled with each week. Rochelle, Joanne, Mrs. Zhang, Pastor Leon, and other familiar faces were in the diner that night. Kim spotted Joanne approaching with a smile as she walked over and took Kim's hand in her own.

"How have you been, girl?" Joanne asked as she released Kim's hand.

"Really good, actually," Kim answered quickly. "Just waiting on my date."

"That's right!" Joanne's face lit up, a widening smirk across her lips. "Wonderful! We can really get to know him. What was his name again?"

"Malik," Kim answered nudging her. "He's bringing his venison chili and I'm just waiting for him to get here."

Looking around at the group of people, Kim wondered if this was going to be too much for him. Since he wasn't much of a socializer, she worried that the crowd of people gathered in a small area could end up being too much interaction for him. Every moment with him was an opportunity to discover more about him and she found herself giddy before they spent time together. Even now, expecting him to show up to the book club for the very first time to meet some of her closest friends had her smiling to herself despite her worry over his social anxieties.

She had spent a lot of time learning about his favorite activities, and he was about to join Kim in one of hers for the first time. Rochelle ran up to Joanne and Kim and gave them each a quick hug. She looked excited, her voice almost echoing in the small space of the diner.

"I love book club days; this is so much fun." Rochelle laughed, turning to Kim. "How are you, dear?"

"I'm great," Kim replied, leaning in so Rochelle could hear her over the others talking around them.

"Oh, that's good to hear." Rochelle raised her finger as if she was going to point at something, but instead, used it as a signal of her remembering. "I almost forgot. I need to go turn down the mac and cheese before it overcooks. I'll be right back, Kim dear. Then we can chat about this boyfriend that's coming to our little gathering. I need all the details." Rochelle patted Kim's shoulder and headed for the tables of food.

"She's a character," Joanne sighed, sipping a drink from a white disposable cup that Kim didn't notice she had before.

Both of Kim's business-owning friends in Sweetgum had differing and yet compatible personalities; they reminded her of the characters in a best friend's movie. They'd probably swoon and crowd Malik when he arrived, thinking of how curiously honest the conversations at book club could be. The book club members spent far more time gossiping and catching up than they did talking over the current novel. With all her time with Malik lately, Kim had hardly had a chance to read it, skimming the pages the few days before.

Kim checked her phone in her pocket for the time. It seemed Malik was running a little late, but Kim knew he'd show up. He wasn't someone who didn't keep his word. At that moment, the jingle of the diner door turned everyone's heads toward the familiar figure of Malik. He stood with his hand around a Tupperware bowl full of chili and a bottle of local wine. The awkward smile on his face practically melted her insides. How could anyone help but to love that face?

"Hey," Kim practically sighed, approaching him with a grin.

Her chest fluttered and her nervousness all but evaporated now that he was here. Sometimes she had to remind herself how quickly life could change. Only a month ago she was on a terrible date that she was unsure she would make it out alive from. And now she was giddy that her boyfriend had just arrived at the book club she attended. Kim rushed over to help Malik with his small offerings, setting down the large, covered bowl on the table next to the other food. She then turned to him, offering a hug and a gentle peck on the cheek.

"Hey to you, too," Malik chuckled, his voice soft in Kim's ear.

Malik's arms hugged her just as tightly as she squeezed him. They had not been apart long but every time it felt like months, and it amplified her longing for him. Breathing against his coat, Kim smelled something musty but sweet like a cologne. It was intoxicating and she wanted to stay within Malik's large arms, but she let go knowing that people would be gawking at the two holding up the food table. He reached over and set the bottle of wine down amongst the other drink options.

Malik looked down at the dish he brought, then back up to Kim with a grimace. "I brought the venison chili."

"I can't wait for everyone to try it." Kim nodded, turning to the gathering swarm of friends.

"You made it!" Joanne slipped between Malik and Kim. She casually reached her hand out and Malik shook it. "I don't know if you remember me, from when you visited my café."

Malik smirked. "Well, I guess I can reintroduce myself. I'm Malik."

Kim was elated to have seen Malik already doing great with people. "Malik, can I show you around a bit?"

Malik nodded in approval. "Well, Joanne, it's nice to see you, again."

"It's nice to see you, too." Joanne winked at Malik.

Kim shook her head and led Malik through the diner of curious but friendly people. She located Rochelle by the counter setting out plastic utensils and paper plates. Kim tapped Rochelle on the shoulder, and she spun around, a smile across her face as her eyes went up to spot Malik.

"You made it!" Rochelle smiled, waving enthusiastically at Malik as she reached out to take his hand. "Hi, welcome."

"Malik, I take it you remember Rochelle?" Kim asked, encouraging them to speak.

"Yes, the very person who led you to me." Malik smiled, glancing at Kim, and then winking. "Without Miss Rochelle, we would have never met."

Rochelle smiled and lightly patted Malik's shoulder. "My goodness. You're really good at making a woman feel complimented."

Kim laughed quietly. "He's good at seeing the bright side of things."

Everyone had basically come to the same idea that Kim's whole woods experience was a thing no one but her date was to blame for. It was slowly becoming something to laugh off and Kim was okay with that. She was mostly over it since someone amazing was brought into her life as the result.

Kim spotted Demetrius behind Malik and shot her arm up to wave him over. "Hey, Demetrius." He headed over to Kim with a sleepiness to his gait.

"Hi," Demetrius answered Kim in his constantly sullen tone. He turned with a nod to Malik, grimacing slightly. "He must be treating you right if he's still around."

"Yes, he is." Kim smirked at the joke. Her eyes met Malik's. "You remember Demetrius from the comic store?"

"Absolutely." Malik gave Demetrius a firm handshake. "How are you?"

"Great, man." Demetrius stared past Malik and Kim at the food table. "I'm going to head over here and get some of Rochelle's famous macaroni and cheese. We'll talk later, all right?"

Rochelle scooted out of the way then spotted someone she wanted to talk to, leaving Kim and Malik alone. Malik moved next to Kim and looked over the crowd as if scanning for anyone he might have known, but Kim wanted more than anything to introduce him to India. As she waited to spot her, Kim noticed the young pastor of the local Baptist church headed their way.

"Leon, hi." Kim shook Leon's hand. "This is Malik, my boyfriend and a local park ranger." Leon was a shorter, thin man with a wide smile and curious eyes, who dressed nicely and smelled like incense. Malik seemed happy to meet him, the two men shaking hands.

"I have heard a great deal about the two of you lately." Leon nodded, greeting him kindly.

"Is that a bad thing?" Malik asked, a bit worried about what this important person might think of them. He hadn't realized that he'd cocked his head a little to the left, staring a bit too intently.

"I don't think so. You helped Kim, so it's a great thing," Leon assured, patting him on his shoulder. Kim knew Malik wasn't very adept in social situations, but Leon didn't seem to catch on. "So, you live in the woods, right?" Leon asked.

"Uh, yeah," Malik answered, shifting on his feet. "It's... quiet."

"What's it like? Do you do a lot out there?" Leon seemed genuinely curious. "I've just never seen you before or at least I don't think I have anyway."

"Yeah, I have a cabin a ways back. I like to hike or take my horse for trail rides. It's peaceful out there." Malik appeared to be getting uncomfortable.

People were probably realizing Malik was a bit of a recluse. Kim sensed the awkwardness settling between the three rather quickly. Thankfully India came striding to the rescue.

"Kim!" India rushed in for her hug with excitement in her voice.

"I'm so glad you're here." Kim hugged India back just as enthusiastic. "I want to finally introduce you." They pulled apart.

"Oh, my goodness." India giggled. "Is this the guy?"

"Yes, India, this is Malik. Malik, this is India, my best friend." Kim waited as they both shook hands.

"It's so nice to finally put a face with the name of the guy Kim won't stop talking about." India lightly nudged Kim with her elbow.

"It's nice to meet you, too." Malik grinned.

Rochelle popped over to the three talking and addressed Kim. "Can I steal Malik for a bit? I want to introduce him to some people."

"Yeah, if that's okay with him." Kim looked to Malik who nodded.

"Great." Rochelle hooked Malik's arm in hers and led him away.

"So, I got caught up talking about you two before coming over here. You guys are a popular topic." India raised an eyebrow to Kim. "Everyone seems to like Malik."

"I'm curious what you talked about." Kim chuckled.

"Oh, mostly if you guys are going to get married in the near future." India's eyes squinted as a smile spread across her entire face.

"What?" Kim almost choked on her words. "That's way too soon." They both laughed hard.

"I really see you guys staying together, like, forever." India gave Kim a gooey look.

"I like him a lot." Kim shrugged, blushing. "Who really knows? Maybe we will end up on the other end of forever."

"He's super interesting in a mysterious kind of way," India admitted, keeping her voice low. "He's tall, sexy, rugged, a bit withdrawn, but then again, so are you. He seems kind and thoughtful. Everyone can see you guys are going to make it."

"I hope so." Kim stared through the crowd at Malik. She really did hope Malik was the one for her.

CHAPTER THIRTEEN

Malik played with his keys in his hands, flipping them over and over as he stood near the Jeep outside Kim's duplex apartment. It was a quiet afternoon for a Friday, there was little happening in Sweetgum and a lull permeated the air. Kim had left work early, having no clients after two and contacted Malik via the ranger station. Lyle was kind enough to radio Malik for her, and in exchange she was to bring him two of his favorite Turkish tea packets and a small jar of granny's blackberry jam.

Malik was grateful for the Jeep but nervous as she came out of her home onto the small front stoop. He came up the sidewalk then, grabbing up her largest backpack and carrying it to the back seat of the vehicle, despite the protests that she was capable of doing it herself. She followed behind him quickly, a smaller back-pack and a cloth grocery sack in her other hands. When he turned to greet her, all form of protest was gone. She paused, tilting her head just slightly to smile at him and plant a soft kiss on his lips.

"Thank you." She smiled, putting her bags in the back seat, and squeezing his arm. "How are you today?"

"Well, the weather is surprisingly warm for February." He shrugged, glancing at a passing vehicle. "How about you? Good morning at work?"

"Mostly uneventful, which is an odd day at work, if I'm honest." She nodded, wrapping an arm around him, and hugging him gently. Her closeness had his chest tightening and his heartbeat quickening, an effect he had found being in her presence. "Is it silly that I missed you?"

"No, I missed you too," he admitted, his heart now thundering in his chest. She must have heard it too because her smile widened brightly, her blush melting his heart as he leaned down to capture those soft, dark lips. She held him closer when he did, his hands going around her protectively as another car passed by.

"We should get back to the park," she finally admitted, pulling away slightly. Kim was somewhat breathless, but the brightness of her blush as his lips lingered over hers had him struggling to pull away.

"Sounds good, do we need to stop anywhere? I grabbed a few items from the store before I got here." Malik pointed, taking a small but effort-leaden step back and pointing to a paper bag in the back seat. "Snacks, coffee, and some milk. I was out."

"I brought a bottle of wine, I hope you don't mind." Kim giggled, allowing him to open the door of the Jeep for her. "I'm just excited for you to show me more. Will you teach me how to hunt? Or track? The plants were really interesting, and I'd like to learn more about finding and identifying them."

"One step at a time," he said with a nod, pushing a braid over her cheek gently before coming around to the driver's seat of the car. Her excitement was rubbing off on him, making him feel like he was a kid again, sitting at his grandfather's feet, learning everything about the wilderness again for the first time. "We'll take the Jeep up the trail as far as it can go and then do a bit of off-roading before I park it."

"Now that sounds like an adventure." She nodded, strapping herself in.

The ride back to the park was full of music from the local radio, excited conversation about the offroad trails, and the improvements Malik made to his cabin. She seemed surprised to hear about the improvements and he had to admit he went a little far. He'd decided to buy a compost toilet for his cabin and a solar-powered shower was installed in his new stone and thatch-panel outdoor shower. It wouldn't be so pleasant in the winter months, but it would be nice the rest of the year. She hadn't complained once about the lack of amenities in his cabin, but he figured she would appreciate it nonetheless.

When they reached the park and ranger station, Kim insisted on getting out and bringing Lyle his tea and jam personally. Their conversation about the weather, her granny, and the upcoming Founders Day celebration in May was eye opening for Malik, as he hadn't participated in any of the town events, holidays, or celebrations since he'd been here. He'd noticed busy and quiet days and knew about the usual holidays like Thanksgiving and Christmas, but he'd never celebrated any of it with locals. Lyle invited him into town every year for holiday celebrations, particularly Christmas, but he refused, preferring the comfort of his cabin on the mountain.

When Kim got back into the Jeep, waving goodbye to Lyle on the porch, Malik noticed a curious look on his boss's face. He wasn't sure if it was a warning or a serious concern, Malik waving weakly as the old man crossed his arms. His mind was quickly distracted by Kim's excitement to take the main trail roads up the mountain and offroad.

"Will we be hiking a lot or are you going to show me more about rock climbing? I was really interested in understanding more," Kim admitted when they had reached the end of the service road atop the bluff overlooking Sweetgum Lake and nature center. "I suppose it is natural for you, since you were taught at a younger age."

"We can go for a hike, and I can show you some fundamentals of rock climbing, but we don't have the equipment out here," Malik explained, smiling over at her as he shifted the Jeep. "Just the emergency equipment in the trunk and my spare sets of hooks and rope at the cabin. However, if you are interested, there is a place twenty minutes away that has a rock wall we can use."

"Really?"

"Yeah, a sporting complex or something." He shrugged, driving over the rough and narrowing trail toward the rocky incline up the next bluff. Kim was excited, smiling and laughing but he could see the fear in her eyes when the Jeep tipped and swayed down the uneven trail. "But don't worry, this Valentine's weekend is about relaxing and enjoying one another's company. I even got some drinks, and I am making us dinner tomorrow night."

"It sounds like an amazing weekend," Kim sighed, something odd in her reaction. "I'm so happy to just be spending time with you, away from everything else."

"Sounds like you need to go fishing." Malik smiled, making it up over the last rocky rise onto the bluff. It was here, amongst the tall cedar and maple, that he stopped and parked the Jeep. He made sure to put the canvas top on, grabbing out the two bags from the back seat and Kim's one extra bag. She insisted she carry more but he refused, stuffing everything that would fit and be safe in the large backpack he strapped on his back.

"Fishing?" she finally asked, after Malik had pointed out the trail leading further uphill to the shallow ravine where his cabin sat.

"Oh, yeah, that's what my granddaddy would always say when there were tough times or my mind was full of worries."

Malik shrugged, leading her up the trail, a smile on her face as she clutched her small bag to her shoulder. "Fishing is the best way to clear the busy mind."

"And do we have the equipment for fishing?" she questioned, following him with a grin. The golden sunlight filtered through the evergreen branches above, giving the entire forest floor a green glow. Kim's smile was radiant in that light as he slowed his pace to be sure she was keeping up.

"I have the poles and lures; we just need the bait." He smiled, climbing carefully up the trail's switchback rises to get to the top where they could just walk along the ridge to the cabin. "The question is, what's buzzing around in your mind that requires a fishing trip to silence?"

"Everything and anything," she admitted, smiling sheepishly at him. "I'm so grateful for my celebrity client and the attention it has gotten me and the salon but I'm struggling with it all. It is just overwhelming sometimes, and on top of it, I've got a co-worker that just doesn't like me."

"Who in this world would dare dislike you?" Malik asked, winking at her slyly as they crested the rise above the Jeep's homemade parking place. He had a hard time imagining someone not enjoying Kim's presence.

"It's my co-worker. Jessica has always been… confrontational," she finally settled, shrugging. "It's not new but it does take a toll after a while."

"I can understand that." Malik nodded, reaching out to take her hand in his gently as they trekked the last ten or fifteen minutes up the mostly flat trail. The leaves rustled overhead, making a rustling sound as their boots scraped against the trail. "I don't get down to the ranger station very often. Lyle's a good man but the other rangers just aren't the kind of guys I'd enjoy spending time with." He remembered the last few times he had tried to join a conversation of theirs at the station. It had ended in confused glances and awkward smiles as he had stumbled over his words.

"No?" Kim asked, squeezing his hand gently, as if sensing his thoughts. "They seem like nice guys and they're both local – I think they were both a couple years older than me in school." A crease formed between her eyebrows as she thought.

"Well, I'm not the most social person in Sweetgum," he admitted, making her smile again. "But I've always liked my life and I'm very picky about who I let into that life." Too many times had he gotten emotionally burned by letting the wrong people into his private life. It was something he had worked never to experience again.

"That might be wise," Kim agreed, allowing him to help her down the small incline toward the meadow and clearing where the roofline of the cabin could be spotted. "But I think you'll find some good friends here in Sweetgum. I was practically raised by the town and though they might go about it in odd or silly ways, people like Rochelle and Joanne and other community leaders mean well."

"They were all way too kind." Malik smiled, leaning over and kissing her forehead before approaching the barn and small fenced pasture. It wasn't really a pasture as it was barely big enough for Hen to roam around, the fencing made of roughly hewn branches and discarded cut pieces. It kept her in the shrub and grass covered clearing of the cabin, but Malik allowed her to roam the trees surrounding it when he was outside doing work and chores.

"I thought they were being a bit rough, to be honest." Kim shrugged, setting down her bag on the cabin's small front porch before following Malik to the barn. "They are all like family and you know how families are when you start dating someone new, mysterious, and unlike anyone they've ever met."

Malik chuckled at this, sliding open both barn doors to let in more light. As he did so, he heard the crunching of hay as Hen twisted around in her stall. He then stepped up onto the ladder and opened a small upper window to let a shaft of light flood through the dusty, and small, barn. Hen was standing there, in her small stable, swaying as she munched on the alfalfa Malik had put in her trough earlier. After sliding open the doors to the pasture, Malik turned back to Kim, still carrying his giant bag on his back.

"What's first, mister mountain man?" she asked, teasing him with a soft kiss.

"How about we find some herbs and take an easy hike?" he offered, wrapping his arms around her waist. "We'll need some herbs for dinner, but I thought you might be interested using them as medication. The natives of this area, the Creek and Cherokee would gather herbs, saps, and barks from these mountains for generations. I thought, maybe, you'd be interested in some local history and skills."

"That sounds great." Kim nodded, kissing his lips gently. "Thank you, I've always been interested in the native history of the area. I'm a donor to the historical society and a frequent attendee and volunteer for their events."

"What events do they do?" Malik asked, leading her to the cabin to put their things away.

"Well, as you know, Founders Day is in May and there is usually a whole week dedicated to it," Kim explained, following him to the front door with her bag again. "And the historical society is heavily involved with the Fall Harvest Festival in September and the Pumpkinfest in October."

"I've been to the markets during fall harvest." Malik nodded, unlocking the door to the cabin, and letting her in. It was dark but after getting her things situated, and opening the wooden shutters, they were both ready to go out on their hike.

It was relaxing, the conversation endless as they took their canteens and small packs further up the mountain. They spoke of childhood adventures, musical loves, college and education, and Kim also told him more about her family's roots and ties to Sweetgum Meadows. Her family was part of the founding of their town, over two hundred years ago, and have been involved in the church, historical society, town council, and conservation efforts. It was amazing to Malik that one family could be the thread that stitched such a friendly community together. As they stopped in a clearing lined with wild berries, Malik explained to her the different types of herbs and plants all around them.

Kim seemed genuinely interested, asking questions about different applications, making oils, and the environment the herbs grew in. He spoke about kitchen herbs as well as various applications of wildflowers and tubers like dandelions and groundnut. He was happy to show her the various plants, Kim insisting on taking photos with her phone and inserting them into meticulous notes as Malik spoke. It was a bit new to him, but he was beyond happy that she wanted to learn and be interested in things he liked and did on a daily basis.

They spoke and laughed, coming up to one of the higher passes and ridge, overlooking the treetops and the vague outline of the ranger's cabin below. You couldn't see the lake or road but when trucks and loggers drove down the main street toward the town, you could see their tops. He and Kim sat up there for a while, discussing plants, various survival tips, and about the upcoming Founder's Day plans. On the way back to the cabin, Malik showed her the snares and traps he set, promising to show her more of them.

That night was quiet, the two of them sitting down to a bottle of local wine and Malik's grandaddy's recipe for roasted and stuffed chicken, and after, Malik taught her how to play gin-rummy. They were laughing, talking, playing the game, and then Kim got out some of her favorite teabags for them to try. He let her stoke the fire, rebuild it, and even showed off his new amenities before dark. She helped him feed the chickens in their coop, settle Hen in, and did dishes before he offered to read her one of his favorite books. A western by Louis Lamour that his grandfather had given him a copy of when he was still in grade school.

Kim agreed thankfully, changing into a pair of comfortable shorts and a long t-shirt, her braids she pinned atop her head. After washing her face, using the newly installed eco-toilet, and brushing her teeth, she was ready to cuddle in bed and listen to the story. She slid into his small bed, motioning for Malik to join her after he changed into a pair of shorts and blew out all the candles leaving one near the bed. The fire crackled, restocked, and warm as the cool February wind whipped and snapped outside. Kim fell asleep in his arms, the story slowing as their hands and lips roamed beneath the sheets.

The next day was even more enjoyable, gathering the eggs and having them for breakfast with fresh dark roast coffee. Malik had decided to show her somewhere special that day, packing a bag, feeding Hen, and then riding further up the mountain together. Kim enjoyed it, holding him close as they set atop one of the highest rises on the mountain that was still accessible via trail. Malik showed Kim how to identify certain trees, landmarks, trails, and he even showed her how to set more traps along the way. She seemed comfortable, at home with the forest and trails, a relief to him as he wasn't sure if she was that kind of person. He felt like he'd do anything for Kim and in that moment, atop the mountain rise, he realized it for the first time. It scared, elated, and humbled him, tears springing to his eyes suddenly, blinking them away before Kim could notice.

They had lunch after gathering some useful herbs, setting some snares, and spotting a small spring and creek in a shallow ravine. It wasn't quiet either, the birds coming back to life in their springtime excitement. The chittering, singing, and calling of birds was only a backdrop to the trickling gurgle of the spring and small stream, lined with moss and black beetles. They enjoyed that small oasis atop the cliff, chatting about the changing of seasons and dreams before Kim insisted on fishing. Malik knew a perfect spot just north of the cabin ridge with a wider, deeper ravine and river.

After returning to the cabin, watering, and allowing Hen to rest, they took off on foot with their poles and packs. Malik carried a large pack with drinks, utensils, some supplies, and the tackle box and strapped the fishing poles into the sack itself. The lures and lines were hooked and didn't dangle but they still jiggled above his head as he walked hand-in-hand with Kim to the river. It was the same river that fed Sweetgum Lake and had the usual freshwater river fish like bass and catfish. They spent twenty minutes hiking up to the main trail that wound around the deeper ravine. The river was high, trickling steadily below as they approached, the snows that fell further up the mountain weeks ago now melting and causing the usual havoc with mudslides and rushing rivers.

They were pleasantly surprised when they did reach the riverside, the rocky and shrub-covered shores ideal for an afternoon together. He taught her what each part was, how to use the hook, and how to properly thread a worm. It turned out that Kim had what his grandfather called "the lure." Luck or natural talent made no difference, Kim had caught a total of three bass, two catfish, and some smaller bull fish that they threw back happily. Malik only caught one fish all day and they both settled on the small feast Malik had prepared back at the cabin.

It was a night of surprises for him, the day fading away as they finished the food he'd prepped earlier that morning. Leaving it over low burning coals all day gave it a deep flavor and when the sunset approached, Malik had one final surprise for his valentine. He'd never spent Valentine's Day with someone like this, his last Valentine's Day celebration turned sour because his girlfriend at the time wasn't really a hiker, like she insisted she was.

Malik led Kim back toward the deeper ravine where the river sat, except this time he stayed atop the ledges, following the tree line until it reached a small rocky crag. There was a stone and dirt trek down into it, not too wide but slowly sloping until it reached another small ledge. It was here that the crag opened up, like a set of jaws, hanging spikes of stone and water dripping above. The small ledge that overlooked the swift drop below was beautiful, the green stretching out below and into the west as the sun set. Malik was smiling in a silly way as Kim took in the small ledge and crag, touching the weeping stones as she followed in into the gaping jaw.

Within was the real surprise, the trickling sound of water and dripping stalagmites adding to the ambiance within. It was a shallow set of waterfalls inside the rock, dripping down and filling small but deepening pools that steered the water toward the river below. Kim was ecstatic, her eyes wide as she saw the meres of water, interconnected by dripping rushes of stone and moisture. She immediately got near, kneeling to feel the clear and stone-filtered water.

"It is a natural cave, created by thousands of years of dripping and flooding waters." Malik grinned, pulling out a small solar lantern and switching it on. The bluish glow made the wet stone twinkle about them as he pulled out a half a dozen candles from the bag he had. She was astounded he had brought those with him. He always talked about how she shouldn't be carrying unnecessary items when she could have brought more food or water. It was possibly one of the most romantic things she had ever had a man do for her.

"You planned all this?" Kim asked, a tear in her eye as she smiled up at him. "Malik, I can't believe it. It's so beautiful and amazing. Thank you."

"It is my favorite place on this mountain, hidden from the

hikers and locals," he admitted, lighting a match, and spreading the candles about on stony ledges and along the floor of the tall wet cave. Drops of water fell from the ceiling sporadically, echoing as they hit the cave floor, making a sort of music. "The water is a bit chilly this time of year, but it's pure, and the pools are shallow enough to keep it temperate. Would you like to try with me?"

"How cold?" she asked, smirking at him. He made his way toward her, taking his sweet time.

"I can keep you warm…"

"Oh?" she asked, standing so she was face-to-face with him finally. "How will you do that?"

"I can think of a few ideas," he admitted, shrugging his shoulders as his arms wrapped around her waist. "What are your ideas? I'm willing to try something new…"

"You're amazing," she sighed, a smirk on her lips as she grabbed his collar.

Their arms roamed one another, shedding clothing and shoes until Malik gently, and carefully, hoisted her into the shallow pool with him. It was the deepest one in the cave, but it barely went above Kim's waist, his hands finding her warm and sensitive skin. They stayed in that cave until after dark, the last rays of sun outside fading as Malik convinced her to head back with him. It was dangerous on the cliffs and hills at night, and he was positive he could continue his efforts back in the warmth and comfort of his cabin.

CHAPTER FOURTEEN

$\mathcal{M}$alik was to meet Kim for lunch that afternoon and then meet her at her place after work so he could stay the next couple nights. Their Valentine's weekend was three weekends ago and Malik was growing surprisingly impatient to see Kim. Every day he'd wake up and his first thought was to wonder what Kim was up to that day. He finally purchased a new cell phone, after his last one had broken over two years ago, and was eager to send a text to Kim whenever he did something that made him think of her.

She would always text him back, either a couple of sentences or emojis, sometimes making him blush with how much she missed him. He was unable to spend the night with her the weekends following Valentine's due to the mudslides, flooding, and spring storms that were becoming more common for the area. Soon, hurricane season would start and that was always a pain. He had hoped to come into town last weekend and spend Friday through Monday with Kim, however, an emergency situation involving missing hikers and a last strong snow on the mountain forced him to stay home.

He had become tired of waiting and hoping to see Kim in his free time. He had been seriously considering moving closer to town over the past few weeks. They'd only been dating a short time, but Malik felt like they could become closer if they could spend more time together. This was becoming difficult as the trek out to his cabin took some special arrangements and more time than he cared to admit. So, with recommendations from Lyle, Malik had spent that morning before meeting Kim for lunch looking at local farm and cabin listings within twenty miles. He'd have to purchase a vehicle, but Lyle offered him his old Ford truck for a few hundred dollars if he was looking at moving. It needed repairs and new tires, but it was a small price for a reliable ride to and from the park.

With that in mind, Malik looked at three listings around town, and five listings that sat within the hills around and south-west of Sweetgum Meadows. Of all the options, the best was a small, old farm home, built over seventy years ago that needed some love and renovations. The lot was decent, comprising six acres of forest and mountain and two acres of yard and pasture. It was a small, but worthwhile investment for himself and his relationship with Kim. He couldn't expect her to wait around for him or make the trek up the mountain every time they wanted to spend time together. It wasn't fair and he was more than willing to leave his remote location for the woman he felt so strongly about. It may not have been his first love, but it was the first time a woman truly tried to understand him and found him worthy of her love and attention. He would do anything to keep himself from returning to his life before, the loneliness of the cabin atop the mountain.

He was waiting for Kim at the diner, Rochelle offering him some of her sweet sun-tea and a piece of pie while he waited. He accepted gratefully, the older woman chatting about a local eccentric he hadn't met when Kim came in, all smiles and sunshine. It was always like this, her presence like the warmth of a good blanket or the late summer sun. She hugged Malik, kissing his lips gently before waving at Rochelle to bring her some tea.

"So sorry I'm late." Kim chuckled, wrapping her arms around his waist tightly. "I missed you so much. How was your morning?"

"Good, I was actually going to tell you about it over lunch." He nodded, sitting back down as she did. "You know what you want to eat?"

"I'll have some of that apple pie, a side-salad, and a butter roll." Kim smirked, looking up at Rochelle who had just set down her tea. "What about you? Just pie?"

"That sloppy joe from the book club was pure flavor," Malik insisted, smiling up at Rochelle. "Can I just get a couple of those sandwiches?"

"Not a problem." Rochelle winked, squeezing Kim's shoulder. "Side of fries?"

"Fried green tomatoes." He smirked, making Rochelle chuckle.

"The boy can eat!" She nodded her approval. "I like him. Fire up the grill, boys!"

Kim giggled as she disappeared back into the kitchen, Malik taking Kim's hand as she sipped her tea through a straw. She seemed confused by the intimacy of the gesture but quickly laced her fingers with his. Malik wasn't sure where to begin and thought it best to just be honest with her, as it was something she had made a point of when they had first started dating.

"You look like you're going to be sick," Kim whispered, leaning into touch his forehead. "Are you okay?"

"I've been looking at houses and rentals in the area," he admitted, unable to stop the blush that rose on his ears and neck. "I'm looking at farmsteads, cabins, and rentals around town because I don't want to make you trek up the mountains every time you want to visit me. I don't want you waiting around for me to show up at your door, either. I… I want us to spend more time together."

Kim watched him for a moment, her bright honey brown eyes not leaving his face as she considered his words. Malik couldn't tell what she was thinking, the confusion, surprise, and shock of his words fading into a delighted grimace. Then she stiffened, biting her lip before leaning back in her chair. Something had settled in her eyes and on her face that resembled anger and annoyance, and Malik braced himself for the worse. He knew it might have been too soon to talk about something like this, and he only hoped she understood where he was coming from.

"What do you mean by rentals?" she asked, her voice soft but her words short.

"I mean rentals, like there is a duplex on Card Street and there is another just outside town past the park that the bank would give me the loan for," he reasoned, feeling the blush and fear grow. "But, if you think it's too much, too fast, then I can wait, see where we go from here…"

"You're so eager to sacrifice," she whispered, leaning closer and taking his hands. "Malik, listen to me. I am more than ready to spend more time with you, and I'd love to have you closer, but I'm not comfortable with you giving up everything you know and love to be closer to me. That's not how I want you to show me love, okay?"

"I don't understand," Malik replied, watching her closely. "Why don't you want me moving closer? I'm willing to move closer, so why are you worried?"

"I care for you, and I've not been serious about any man in a long time," she admitted, her blush brightening. "And I don't want my man sacrificing everything he is to satisfy a want that doesn't really exist. I want to stay with you in your cabin, to learn about the woods, and fish, and plants, and snares and everything else!"

The few patrons in the diner glanced over at her raised voice and Rochelle peeped from behind the counter, but otherwise the two sat there in stunned silence. Malik wasn't expecting her to be angry about this and he definitely wasn't prepared for what she said. It made Malik wonder what she was trying to prove to him, and his eyes narrowed, making her pause.

"I don't want to upset you, but I still don't fully understand what you're saying," he admitted, his voice low again as he laced his fingers with hers again. "What is it that you want to do?"

"I want to spend more time at the cabin, and I want you to spend more time here, in town," she explained, pulling his hand gently. "I want us to understand one another on equal terms."

"Equal terms?"

"Yes, you amongst the wild berries, waterfalls, and mountains but also here, with me, being involved with the community and friends." Kim smiled, stroking the top of his hand with her thumb. "I... am worried that you are isolating yourself, pulling away from people instead of embracing them."

"I like some people," he admitted, making her chuckle. "But I know what you mean. I see you learning, I see you becoming stronger, but I'm afraid you'll hurt yourself trying to gain what it took me a lifetime to earn. Life off-grid, life on a homestead, is hard work and a lot of sacrifice... I just didn't want you to have to sacrifice more than what's fair."

"Is that what you're worried about?" she asked, leaning close and kissing his lips gently. "That I'm sacrificing too much for our relationship?"

"You are learning to trap, fish, and rock climb." He smirked, kissing her gently. "Is there another handsome park ranger whose caught your fancy or is that all me?"

"It's *all* for you," she sighed, squeezing his hands. "Because I want to be there for you, to help you, to encourage you, and most importantly, I want to understand you. I want to understand Malik."

"But are we… on the same level here?" he asked, a bit breathless at her confession.

"I care deeply for you, and I want to spend more time with you. Isn't that the level we are on?" she asked, smirking at him.

"I've never felt this way about a woman," Malik explained, placing his hand on her face softly. "I want you all to myself, but I need the world to see your warmth, your beauty, and your talent. I want to spend days, no, years talking to you about everything and then wake up and do it all over again. You're an amazing woman, Kim…"

"Then we have to do our best to nurture one another," Kim explained, touching his hand on her cheek. "And I won't hear any more about you moving into town. You'll stay on the mountain you love, and I will introduce you to the people I love."

"Who haven't I met?" he asked, glancing at Rochelle who was approaching with their meals and a pitcher of sweet tea.

"Here you are." She smirked, winking at Kim as she set down the warm plates. "Are we going to see you at book club next week, Malik?"

"Yes, and I'd like to volunteer for Founders Day," he explained, nodding excitedly at the prospect of meeting more of Kim's friends.

"Wonderful, I'm sure your granny and father will be thrilled." Rochelle nodded, turning back to the other customers. Her words had sent a shot of ice straight down Malik's spine, realizing that he had yet to meet any of her family.

"You okay?" she asked, noticing he hadn't started eating yet.

"I haven't met your parents," he said, staring at the plate in front of him. "I hadn't even considered that as it was never really an issue for me. I… what is your father's name? What about your mother? Do you have siblings?"

"Relax." Kim smiled, nodding at his food. "Eat, breathe, and we'll discuss all that tonight over dinner. I'm making granny's fried chicken so don't you eat anything after this until dinner."

"Yes, ma'am." He smirked, both of them digging into their food like hungry animals. Malik appreciated Kim's honesty and her kindness, something he was sure to need again in the future. This girl was so smart, so ambitious, and so talented that he wondered if it was him that was struggling to keep up with her.

CHAPTER FIFTEEN

Kim was becoming more interested in what Malik was teaching her. She was adamant to be shown more about gathering, setting snares, hiking, and other general things that Malik had been teaching her. She was getting restless and found herself Googling outdoorsy stuff and plant names when she was alone. The library was a good place to start, but the internet had a wealth of information that had not been published in physical books. As much as she loved holding a book in her hands, she was more focused on getting as much information as possible.

Still having a couple books from the library that actually interested her, Kim sat on her living room floor reading on her belly with her legs swaying side to side. She didn't mind it lacked adventure or anything she was typically into reading. It was supposed to be informative, and boy was it. There was even a section about skinning according to the index in the front of the book.

Kim's phone vibrated on the coffee table loud enough to hear. She sat up and flipped it, looking at the notification on the lock screen. India was asking Kim to meet up with her for coffee. Kim quickly replied, 'Be there shortly,' then threw on her shoes. She tucked her phone in her pocket and headed out, leaving the books behind.

Kim entered the café and immediately spotted India who smiled and waved her over. There weren't too many people there, as the early morning rush with people heading to work was over.

"Hey, you." India sipped from a glass cup.

"Hi." Kim smiled. "So, what's up?" She sat across from India.

"Okay, I know you don't care for parties, but I totally want you to come to my birthday bash next weekend." India paused as though finding a way to convince Kim it'd be more fun than she was thinking. "Bring Malik, too, he's invited. It'd be fun for you guys."

"Where are you having it at?" Kim ordered her coffee in between talking. "I'd love to go; I just need the details."

"It'll be at the convention center in town and it's going to have a DJ, of course dancing, drinks, and tons of people, oh and a huge potluck-style dinner, and some silly little games with some prizes." India's excitement was radiating through her words.

"Oh, wow, that does sound impressive. I can't wait. I'll tell Malik and see if he's up for it." Kim got her coffee and sipped on the hot fluid. "He should be up for it."

"Yay! I'm ready for this party!" India finished her coffee. "I'm off to take care of some last-minute preparations. Call me after you ask him. I'll message you later or something." India stood up.

"I will." Kim watched her best friend leave the café with a small hop in her step.

Beyond excited to tell Malik, Kim finished her coffee and booked it home. As soon as she ran inside, she cleaned up some of the clutter she'd accumulated while reading earlier that morning. Malik was supposed to be there soon. She didn't want to call him and appear too eager, so she waited patiently. As the afternoon began to roll around a knock came at Kim's door. She peeked outside and saw it was Malik. She immediately let him in. She took his bag and sat it next to the couch then hugged him hard.

"Well, aren't you in a good mood." Malik's deep voice was light and cheerful.

"It's your first weekend here. And I have something I want to talk about." Kim sat on her couch and Malik joined her, close.

"What's it about?" Malik asked quizzically.

"India, my best friend, is having a party for her birthday." Kim went into the same details India gave her.

"Kim, I can't." Malik appeared worried about something.

"What do you mean? Are you busy that weekend?" Kim sensed something was off, but not sure what.

"No, I don't have any plans. I just don't want to go," Malik admitted with hesitation.

"Why not?" Kim stared at Malik, confused.

"I just don't." Malik stood up and paced slowly. "I can't do it."

"There's a huge difference between can't and won't. What is the problem?" Kim's voice filled with agitation, but she didn't mean for it to. This seemed to upset Malik.

"I'm not going to a party with over a hundred people." Malik kept his voice down, but sterner.

"Look, I know you don't get out much, but it would mean the world to me if you were there." Kim stood up across the room from Malik. "What's wrong?"

"You don't get it. I can't handle that many people." Malik was trying his best not to raise his voice, but it didn't bother Kim. She just wanted to understand.

"I'm here for you. All you have to do is tell me why." Kim spoke softly. Malik plopped on the couch as if defeated.

"I never grew up around people. I don't know what to do around them, especially that many people. You guided me through the book club, but that was a small get together. College was hard and people can be cruel to others," Malik admitted softly.

"I understand, and I'll still be there to help you. I want to help you." Kim sat next to Malik and put a hand on his shoulder. "I used to think I'd never be able to socialize like I do now, even then I barely get out to big events. All it takes is a little bit of confidence. You will be surprised at the things you can do if you tell yourself, you can do them."

"I don't know," he sighed, their eyes meeting.

"I want to help you succeed. I want to be there to watch you grow as a person. You can do this. I'll be right there the whole time, I promise," she said softly. Kim wanted to hug Malik badly. To tell him that it didn't have to be miserable for him. That he could have fun with people and not feel so alone.

"You really think so?" Malik sighed.

"Yes, Malik, I really do." Kim breathed nervously. "If nothing else, you should know that I would never hurt you, or let anyone else hurt you. To be honest... I love you." Malik's eyes softened and his mouth was slightly agape as he looked back at her.

"You do?" Malik asked.

"Yes." Kim smiled shyly, unsure if it was too much or too soon. She didn't want to scare him, and she didn't want him to think she had just said it to make him feel better. In truth, she'd been feeling it more and more recently, that familiar butterfly that propels you toward your lover's arms had become something else. It had become closeness, intimacy, understanding, and passion, something she hadn't been prepared for.

"I love you, too," he replied, reaching out to her, their closeness warm as she buried herself in his embrace.

The music was loud as Kim and Malik strolled up to the convention center. He had taken the Jeep back into town and got ready at Kim's before driving over to the party. India was not lying about her party, the elaborate colorful and glittering decorations lining the main doorway only part of the fun. There were dozens of cars in the lot, and it seemed everyone had gotten held up in the main hallway leading to the hall where most of the town's local events took place.

"Looks like she's already causing drama." Kim chuckled, waving to a woman he hadn't met yet. She waved them through, and they pushed passed the bouncers and security to the curtained hallway beyond. The hallway they were just in was decorated with streamers, glittering flags, and balloons, but the one behind the curtain was all business.

Kim had worn a beautiful blue dress that hugged her curves and fell just below her knees, her golden heals glimmering in the lights as she looked over her best friend's outfit. India was within, standing amongst performers, makeup artists, waiters, and various friends. The birthday girl was dressed in an elaborate black and red dress with a crown on her head, her hair interlaced with braids and curls in a way Malik had never seen before. India waved, spotting Malik and Kim instantly and letting out an excited greeting before wrapping Kim in her arms.

"I was wondering where you were." She laughed, hugging Malik as well. "You look great! Both of you... what's your drink of choice?"

"Sam Adams?" Malik smiled, taking one of the beers from India's friend holding a bucket of ice and refreshments. He was wearing something simple, with a nice tie that Lyle had lent him. It wasn't fancy, simple blue and gold tie to match Kim—she had insisted.

"I'll take a cooler for now." Kim nodded, putting it in her pocket. "So, is everyone here? Do we know?"

"Everyone and then some," she laughed, raising her glass of wine. "The whole town is here and I'm excited to get this show on the road! You've both been placed at the table of honor with me and my lovely sister who didn't even bother introducing herself to your new man!"

The woman that waved them through just waved back, making Kim laugh and India grumble. Malik was so busy taking in the performers and the choir dressed in colorful clothing that he missed their conversation entirely. That was all right, the two laughing and chatting as he looked over the elaborate decorations and the catering that was about to be brought out for the waiting guests in the hall beyond. He could hear the bumping music, the loud chatter, and laughter as he stood there in the barely decorated hallway.

"Come on," Kim insisted, motioning for him to follow. "We're going to miss the performance back here. Let's get our seats and get ready for some delicious food, drinks, dancing, and music."

"Wow, you're really excited." He smiled, squeezing her hand as he followed. "I'm just grateful to be invited but still entirely too nervous. Did she say we were sitting at their table? That's a lot of eyes…"

"Nonsense!" she laughed, poking him with her elbow. "You're my man and you are more than welcome here. You're also a mystery man, which will work to your advantage. Never fear my love, you've got me."

With a soft kiss she led him through another swinging door into the atrium beyond, a whole herd of people lining up, checking costumes, and makeup. He was so confused and excited that he almost spilled his beer on an elaborately dressed woman outside the main doors to the party within. It was staggering, the brightness of the lights swaying on the ceiling with a shining ball of light dangling in the center. The dance floor was sectioned off, tables surrounding it as people took their seats. They were all so nicely dressed, Malik wondering if his simple slacks and collared shirt was enough.

Kim pulled him through the crowds of looking eyes taking their seats at one of the smaller round tables, while Kim led him to a raised square table overlooking the dance floor and small stage near the back of the hall. It was amazing, blues, greens, and yellows pulsing with light and decoration all around them with the music, an upbeat groove of old soul and R&B, contenting the guests.

It wasn't all there was, the two of them reaching their designated and marked seats at the end of the large square table. There was a huge seat in the center, most likely for India, and flanking this chair on the right was a man wearing a black crown. He waved at Kim, who smiled back, and then nodded to Malik politely. Next to him sat another man Malik didn't know and then Kim and he sat on the end after him. On the opposite side of the chair sat an older woman, a couple Malik recognized from the Chinese place, and the sister who had finally taken her spot.

The lights flashed then, everyone whispering, gasping, and

buzzing with excitement as they found their permanent seats. To say that India was extra was a bit of an understatement, her birthday kicking off with a literal bang. Drummers, dancers, fire eaters, and contortionists all came dancing into the room with bright outfits, the music picking up as the curtains beyond revealed the woman of the hour. India sat atop a chair turned throne, carried by four men who laughed, yelled, and chanted as they danced. Then, they brought her to the raised table, setting the chair down on the small, raised stage and pretending to worship her.

There was cheering, laughing, and people were singing along with the music, dancing in their chairs or standing in the back. Malik was curious about the choice of music, but was entertained by the show, which lasted for another few minutes before India stood in front of her chair, ready to make a speech.

"As you all know, I've never been the kind of person to go all out for my birthday!" she said, one of the performers handing her a microphone. "But this year, we've made an exception. I've invited everyone who ever mattered to me and even now, there are people crashing the party!"

She pointed to the back of the hall, everyone laughing and joking as she continued. Her speech was interesting, commemorating the achievements of the past year including her job and buying herself a new car. She also mentioned her boyfriend, the man in the black crown nodding at her and blowing kisses gently. She smiled and giggled at this, winking at him, and mouthing the words "I love you" before returning to the business at hand.

"Now, let's eat this five-course feast provided by the lovely miss Rochelle and the cake was baked by the lovely Joanne Clanton at the Roasted Beans Coffee Spot!"

There was applause, yelling, whistling, and then the food came out from the double doors, flooding the room with a family-style feast on every table. On the main table, where India was laughing, drinking, and enjoying her lavishly over-the-top party, there were plates of fried chicken, beef ribs, macaroni and cheese, potato salad, and baked beans. Along with two or three pies and the main cake, a decorated colorful explosion, the table was weighted down by so any drinks and foods that it was impossible to see the clean white linen underneath.

Malik was thoroughly impressed, everyone laughing, joking, eating, and the entertainers performing over two hours before the DJ came on to take over the dance floor. It was amazing, and the whole time, Malik was getting to know Kim, her friends, and the town she loved even better. So many people came up and talked with him, spoke with him, and even urged him to try some dancing, something Kim and India were enjoying immensely with their drinks and friends. Malik didn't mind, chatting with India's boyfriend Nate, Pastor Leon, Rochelle and her date, Joanne, India's sister Nevaeh, and Mr. and Mrs. Zang.

He had to admit that his expectations of their personalities, and his assumptions, were quite wrong, and he often found Kim smiling at him from the dance floor as he shared a beer or a conversation with someone she knew. Malik would wave at her but this last time, he noticed India was waving, motioning for him to come out on the dance floor. Frightened, caught like a deer in the headlights, he forced himself to move, dismissing himself from Pastor Leon and Rochelle as he sauntered out onto the dance floor.

"There he is!" India smiled, both she and Kim clearly drunk. The party had started over three hours ago and he was glad to see that Kim was happy drunk and not falling-on-the-floor drunk.

"Do you dance?" Kim asked, her eyes wide with hope. "I don't think I've ever asked you that..."

"I've never actually learned," he admitted, shrugging. "But if you want me to move to the beat and pretend, I can try."

"That's the spirit!" India smiled, she and Kim sandwiching him as the beat picked up for the next song.

Malik laughed, held up his beer so he didn't splash it on them, and enjoyed the short, but silly, dance. India insisted he stay for a little longer and he agreed, taking Kim in his arms as he swayed gently and spontaneously to the beat. He'd never done anything like this before, and he didn't know how to dance other than to hold someone close to you and sway like in middle school. That wasn't good enough and so he joked with Kim, laughing as the two of them found their own rhythm. Eventually, they were the only two that mattered, and Malik felt comfortable laughing and getting them all new drinks when the last song was over.

Malik was already buzzed, his mind fuzzy when he saw an unknown man smiling, dancing, and trying to touch Kim. Malik was about to react but saw the annoyance and fury in Kim's eyes as she rounded on the unknown younger man. She squared her shoulders, told him to back off, and explained that she was taken. She was polite but brutally honest, telling him he'd find greener grasses with someone his own age. Malik just watched with pride, slowly walking over with four fruity drinks, offering one first to India, who smiled proudly, and then to the other two girls who were backing Kim up. The younger man glared in Malik's direction before turning around with his friends to talk to some other women across the dance floor. Malik only nodded at Kim, offering her the drink and a kiss on her cheek when she finally turned back from berating the stranger.

It was an hour, and four more drinks later, that he and Kim were sitting in the corner, talking and feeding one another left-over donut holes. Joanne had extras from the crazy colored birthday cake decoration and Kim and Malik were seeing who could catch the most in their mouth. It was fun, Kim catching one but falling out of the chair with a thump and a laugh. The two were giggling, talking to passersby, and evaluating India's extreme state of inebriation when Kim turned to him, her brow knitted in thought.

"What?" he asked, looking for a disapproving glance or an approaching townsperson.

"Let's sneak out of here and get some candy and cocoa." She nodded, moving to stand. She was shaky, finding her balance as she swayed in place – Malik stood to steady her, and they both ended up bracing each other. After giggling, composing themselves, and waving at India, they went out to the hallway where they could hear better.

"Leaving already?" India asked, her arm over her sister Nevaeh's shoulder.

"We're going to go to the store, to get some cocoa and candy, and walk back to my place," Kim insisted, pointing at the clock above them. "It's almost one in the morning!"

"The convenience store is open 24 hours." India chuckled, hugging Malik. "But go, wander home to the love nest. I've got a party to clean up and food to get rid of."

"I'll stop by tomorrow!" Kim promised, hugging her friend tightly. "Save whatever you got, and I'll take some tomorrow."

"Oh, I'm taking all the ribs and mac and cheese," Nevaeh explained, waving her hand. "You can have the baked beans and chicken if you'd like…"

"I'll take em." Malik nodded, admitting that food did sound tasty in his drunken state.

The three women laughed, nodding their approval and hugging him before sending both he and Kim on their way. Malik was truly content, comfortably walking with one arm around Kim's waist across the parking lot, speaking loudly and happily until they spotted the convenience store right around the corner. Kim spoke cheerfully to the clerk, a friend from high school working third shift while studying during the day for her degree. Malik was happy to chat, buy some cocoa for each of them, and his favorite candy – Andes Mints.

They drunkenly chatted for what seemed like hours, but it had only been twenty minutes and Kim was more than ready to go back to her place to relax and get out of her heals. Malik offered to carry her on his back, and she was tempted to take him up on it, but the two just strolled hand-in-hand across the main street, a few blocks over where Kim's street intersected with Central. Her duplex was only two blocks north and Malik was happy to talk with her about her friends, the party, and the upcoming book club.

It wasn't long before they were sauntering up her cleanly cut sidewalk to the stoop and old cedar front door. Kim was giggling, unlocking the door shakily before dragging Malik inside, her hands around his waist desperately. He didn't deny her and, for the first time since they started dating, he felt truly comfortable in her home and amongst her friends.

CHAPTER SEVENTEEN

Kim dug the tips of her shoes onto the rocks jutting out, grabbing the rocks above her on the climbing wall. She was getting better at getting ahold of the smallest ones but sometimes her shoes still slipped on them. She had figured out there were ways to strategically climb the wall while avoiding falling. It was a small wall, but she cheered for herself when she reached the top. Malik smiled at her from below.

"You're getting faster," Malik hollered up to Kim. "Rappel back down here so I can properly congratulate you."

Just like Kim had practiced with Malik a few times, she turned her back to the edge of the small cliff while holding tight to the neon rope. She leaned her butt over the edge first and then her whole body while keeping her footing. She teetered over and began walking backwards down the wall, feeling the weight of her body held by the rope. It was nerve-wracking at first, but muscle memory kicked in after the first few steps.

Kim planted her shoes at the bottom and relaxed her grip on the rope. She released it when Malik swooped in for a big hug. The moment could last Kim a lifetime and she still felt Malik holding her as he released back slightly. He lifted his hand to Kim's chin and pressed under it to lift Kim's head to kiss her lips. Malik's face was warm against Kim's and his lips were soft. His kiss was sensual and relaxed Kim while also creating a fast-passing euphoria.

"You're amazing." Malik brushed Kim's stray hair from her face that had escaped her braids and tucked it behind her ears.

Kim smiled and watched as Malik gathered up the climbing gear and packed it away in his bag. He threw it over his shoulders and reached out for Kim's hand. She took it, intertwining her fingers between his. Kim pulled out her camera with her free hand and held it against herself to turn it on and film the scenery back. They took the familiar path towards Malik's cabin, walking in unison and keeping somewhat close to each other's sides. Malik suddenly stopped short and leaned to the side of the trail. He let go of Kim's hand, puffing like he was irritated.

"What's wrong?" Kim followed him to the trail's edge.

Malik kicked at the weeds with his boot. That was when Kim saw it. There was a bunch of leftover food thrown around with wrappers and what looked like used napkins. Malik grabbed up a small store bag that was lying next to the mess and started to pick up the food with a look of disgust across his face.

"People drive me crazy up here. They can't leave food out here like this. It will attract bears and then it won't be safe on the trails. They'll expect more food and even stalk hikers. It's rare to be attacked but it can happen if people don't stop littering their food. Not to mention that if the bears eat all this junk, it could make them sick." Malik finished picking up the mess then wiped his hand on his pants and tied up the bag.

Still filming, Kim thought about how amazing and cute it was that Malik cared so much about the bears and the environment. Maybe not so much about the people, but he obviously didn't want anyone being attacked. Neither did Kim. She loved

Malik even more watching him through the camera lens protecting the creatures and forest.

"I just wish people would take the time to at least pick up after themselves. There are always warnings on the sites about animals in the area and even in town there are fines for littering." Malik's face was turning red. "Is there any way to get people to understand easier or to even listen?"

Kim opened her mouth to answer but stopped, spotting a rustling in the bushes and trees behind him. Before she could speak, Malik reacted, turning to spot the rustling, and taking a few steps back toward Kim. There, rooting through the bushes and undergrowth was a bear, its long nose and black face turning to stare at them both. It was large, but even Kim could see it was fresh out of hibernation and hungry. Malik froze, his hands slowly rising in the air.

"Kim, do as I do and face the bear," he insisted, his body tense and ready to react at the slightest movement from those black beady eyes. "Be big and do exactly as I say."

"Yes," she responded, instinctually ready to run, climb, or do anything Malik asked of her. Her hands were up, her phone still poised in her fist, unable to really think about anything other than the bear in front of them. It had stopped digging around and looked up, noticing them. It raised part of the way up, standing on its two hind feet, the third pressed against the tree as it sniffed in their direction. Its movements were so swift for its size and Kim's heart pounded in her chest, heat rising to her skin.

Malik stood facing the bear, his arms up and his voice loud as he yelled and faced it, standing right in its path. She was panicking, her hands shaking as she saw the bear drop down with a grunt and take a few too-quick steps forward. It started growling as it came through the trees, the sound echoing through the forest. The bear wasn't deterred by Malik's voice or his movements, coming forward aggressively as Malik reached for his pocket. It all happened so fast that Kim didn't know what to think. The bear swatted at the dirt, lowered its head, and charged. Kim heard Malik scream "run" and she did, turning and fleeing as fast as she could back down the trail.

She made it quite a ways down the path before she heard Malik call her name, saying it was safe to stop running. She paused, looking around her meticulously, afraid to stop at all in case the bear was close behind. She saw Malik jogging toward her, his face panicked, but she saw no bear, his eyes wide as he slowed to inspect her.

"Are you okay?" he asked, touching her face. "It's gone, ran away… I used bear mace."

"I… I'm fine… just a lot of adrenaline and fear," she replied, touching his face between her hands. "We're safe? It's okay?"

"Let's get back to the cabin, but yes we should be all right," he insisted, wrapping an arm around her protectively as they walked back down the trail.

When they finally reached the cabin, Kim relaxed her muscles, getting herself some of her tea and couldn't stop touching and hugging Malik. He seemed to understand, the both of them just holding one another. She didn't know how long they'd sat like that but eventually they were able to separate to get food, more hot tea, and Kim finally was able to check her phone.

It had been recording until the moment she stopped running and Malik found her again. It was good footage of the bear, what he did to deter it, including spraying the mace, and it was ironic since the video began with him talking about leftover food for predators. After showing it to Malik, she told him she wanted to upload it on her social media account but then a great idea came to mind.

"How about we make you a profile as a ranger? To give advice and upload informative videos and stuff?"

"Upload online? Me?" Malik asked, making them both some sandwiches.

"It's pretty important and it's ironic that you find discarded food by inconsiderate hikers." She pointed out, hoping he'd understand her point. "And then what shows up? A bear! I got it all on video…"

"I guess but I don't understand how it's going to help." He shrugged, waving at her. "But go for it, it can't hurt."

"It could be a stepping-stone to more awareness and perhaps some more efforts toward conservation here on our reserve." She shrugged, playing with the video stills and shots.

"You're fascinating, optimistic, and a fast learner." He grinned, kissing her lips one more time before setting down some food and fresh vegetables on the table for dinner.

"You wait, I'll have you online quicker than you got me out here hiking," she promised, kissing his cheek with a giggle as she sat at the table, pouring them both some tea. Kim enjoyed his twinkling dark eyes, jokes about bears, and the pure ecstasy of appreciating him and his warmth.

CHAPTER EIGHTEEN

$\mathcal{M}$alik could feel the nerves building inside him, tightening like coils, ready to spring the moment Kim turned on that camera. Kim, however, sat him down on her couch, cuddled up next to him, and showed him her phone. She explained the basics of what a YouTube channel was and how social media could bring in viewers. Malik didn't care about the revenue earned from ads or the idea of making revenue at all. He would rather people just donate directly to their local rangers and conservationists.

"You see? This is a profile you can post pictures, videos, and status updates," she showed him, pointing to the empty bar where he was supposed to pour out his soul.

"I'm not sure about this," he admitted, glancing out her clean white-paned window. "I don't want to be some face for wildlife or some poster-boy for conservation issues on the internet."

"You might end up as a meme, but I don't see you being the next Steve Erwin or something…"

"Great," he sighed, shaking his head. "I think we should just drop it. Other people can make posts and pictures and videos about trees and stuff. I'm not made for camera…"

"Says who?" she asked, placing her palm against his cheek. "You're beautiful, inside and out."

"I don't know how this is going to go but I guess I just don't care what random people on the internet think." He shrugged, making her chuckle. "So, we'll give it a try, but I mostly want people to understand that their everyday carelessness is just unacceptable."

"Don't worry, I'll help you with everything." She nodded, kissing his lips gently. That night the two set up a couple of social media pages, posted some facts about camping safety and the ecological impacts of plastic, and took some fun pictures of him for the pages. Kim even braided his hair, the two laughing, talking, and listening to music as Kim put a couple of small but tight braids just over his ears, pulling the hair from his face.

The next day the two went out to the park, Kim bringing along her phone and extra battery pack. Malik was still nervous, but Kim encouraged him, guiding him through the various things he could post to gain a following. The idea of him doing his videos shirtless was amusing but would undoubtedly distract from the eco-message he was hoping would catch attention.

On the hike, Kim had him stop a few times to get something she called b-roll footage and Malik felt so awkward. She would take photos of cigarette butts, plastic, rubber, and other random graffiti on the park tables, benches, and trail markers. She also took videos and pictures of Malik as he checked garbage and recycling containers along the trails. He was constantly aware of her eyes and the camera on him, and it was irritating him so much that at one point, he stopped, looked directly at the camera, and crossed his arms stubbornly. Kim grinned but understood, lowering the device, and placing it back in her pocket.

"Sorry," he sighed, shaking his head. "But I just don't think this is going to work."

"It's okay, we don't have to film anymore," Kim assured, smiling kindly. "I noticed you've been tense this whole time."

She motioned for him to join her, sitting down on a nearby set of rocks alongside the main trail. The evergreens above were swaying in the slight breeze and the two of them just sat, enjoying the smells of the pine forest floor. It was quiet for a moment, Malik wrapping an arm around her as they enjoyed one another's company. The chirping of nesting birds, skittering, and fighting squirrels, and the occasional rustle of larger animals in the brush was like music backdropped by the rustle of pine branches above.

"I know this might not help your nerves, but you should try to treat the camera like it isn't even there." Kim smiled, leaning against his shoulder. "Just... pretend you're teaching and explaining to just me."

"I do enjoy teaching you," he admitted, shrugging. "But I like it because I can see you progressing, becoming more comfortable out here with me."

"And I appreciate it," she admitted. "I'm enjoying it a lot more than I thought I would. It's kind of odd... but I've been trying to find a balance for the both of us without realizing that it's become easier with every step."

"I've surprised myself as well." He chuckled, kissing her forehead softly. "Your friends and the people in town are truly good people and I want to spend more time with them and you. I didn't think I'd ever feel that way about people, strangers really, but... well, we've both changed."

"I've seen it." She chuckled, kissing his cheek, nuzzling his neck. "So, why don't we try a bit more filming before we head back down the mountain?"

"All right, I'll try it your way." He smirked, taking her hand gently and leading her up the trail.

The hike up to the next picnic area of the trail and the bluff overlooking the lake below was easy but the mess at the site was irritating. Malik hadn't even realized Kim was filming him, explaining what microplastics, rubber, and garbage in general did to the ecosystem and animals around the area. He was angry but he knew people's complete disregard and inconsiderate attitudes wouldn't change because he complained about it on the internet. It would take more than shame and irritation to change people's minds about littering.

They got so much footage, and Malik was having such a good time explaining his position, that neither of them realized they'd reached the ends of the park trails and were getting into the off-trail locations. The incline up the game and rock climber's trails was becoming steep as they chatted, filmed, took photos for social media but also for themselves. Soon, they approached a cliff and ravine that's rocky faces were more challenging than most of the surrounding trails and climbs. Malik knew of this, but Kim was staring in fascination.

She'd been climbing at the sports center but also on small cliffs near the cabin with Malik. It was fun but she wasn't ready for something this big. However, the excitement and wonder in her eyes caught him off guard as she turned to point at the cliffs above.

"We have to climb that," she insisted, smiling at the rocks above. "It would be great footage for the channel!"

"I've climbed it a few times before, but you are not quite there yet," he admitted, feeling a bit sheepish for bursting her bubble. "It can be climbed in a couple hours, but it is tricky and not for the inexperienced."

"I think we can do it." Kim nodded, the pleading tone tugging at him. "We can take it slow and careful..."

"You're a fast learner, and you've yet to make any serious mistakes," he admitted, wrapping his arms around her with a smirk. "But it'd be irresponsible of me as a ranger and your boyfriend."

"It would really help me out to get some pictures for my

social media too," she explained, swaying there with him as her hands wrapped around his own waist. "I'll do my hair special for the climb, take some pictures along the way, and when we get to the top, I can get some fashion and stylized shots."

"When would we do this?" he asked, smirking down at her. "You really want to climb a mountain for photos on the internet?"

"Absolutely." She laughed, kissing him again. "And we can do it whenever we've got the time."

"Fine, maybe next weekend if we're careful and the weather is ideal." He nodded, both of them laughing as Kim took photos of the small bluff below.

Malik could feel the warmth of her excitement and appreciation flooding through him. His heart warmed when she smiled, when she was happy, and when she mastered the skills Malik had been showing her. She was the most amazing person he had ever met, and he felt extremely grateful to be the one she could rely on.

He hadn't had anyone like that since his granddaddy passed and he hadn't realized how much he missed this feeling of hope and companionship. Since that hopeless day on the mountain in New Hampshire, he'd decided to push it away, to distance himself, and forget hope, something he'd almost given up on entirely.

CHAPTER NINETEEN

It wasn't a typical Thursday morning for Kim, heading to work early as she grabbed her kit and large purse. She was seeing her celebrity client later today to design and work on the braids and wanted everything to go smoothly. She had to make sure her station was clean, comfortable, sanitary, and that all her items were in place and ready for use. She didn't want to risk putting a single hair out of place for this famous YouTuber and music celebrity.

Kim was sure she'd be the first one there to open up, the key hidden very creatively in the windowsill planter under the small, realistic, mossy rock. No one would even think to find the small key there hidden amongst the flowers and rocks but Kim and the other trusted hairdressers, including Jessica, knew of it. When she got to the front door, she was amazed to find it unlocked and the lights within on. Someone had already started their day and she wondered if maybe her boss came in early for the same reason she did. It was her shop after all, and she was a very meticulous woman.

The owner couldn't have been there long, disarming the alarm and only turning on the single dim overhead ceiling fan.

Kim stared around, bags in hand as she looked for a sign of her boss and saw that the backroom lights were on and there was the sound of opening bottles and boxes. Kim strode towards the backroom and came around the corner through the small hallway to find that it wasn't her boss at all.

Her heart stopped dead.

"What are you doing?" Kim asked, her eyes wide.

Jessica was standing over the sink with Kim's open box of extra supplies on the table next to her. She had a tube of braid cream in one hand and a conditioning cream in the other, squeezing them both into the sink. The box of supplies must have just been open as there was no sign of any other emptied bottles or tubes. Kim was furious, instinctually reaching out for the box. Jessica saw who it was and didn't even have the humility to look ashamed. She sneered angrily and threw the tubes back in the box, covered in cream and half full.

"What is your problem!?" Kim snapped, taking her bags and box directly to her station. She was so livid she didn't even hear Jessica's threats fully as the girl lashed out and whined about something or other. Her complaints were nonsensical and unrelated, and Kim had no idea what she was talking about. Kim turned around after she'd secured her items in the drawers, Jessica still standing near the hallway entrance talking at her.

"You can tell the boss and everyone else whatever you want, but it's your word against mine and I know how quickly rumors spread in this small town," Jessica threatened, hands on her hips. Her voice was venom, her eyes narrowed hatefully. "I've got just as many followers as you. Just because you can braid doesn't mean you can do everything! You're not some genius or something."

"What are you talking about?" Kim asked, eyes narrowed as she crossed her arms. She was tired of the drama, the childish games, and the stress. She didn't care what Jessica thought she was doing; Kim wanted an explanation she could understand.

"I'm telling you that if you snitch on me to the boss or anyone else, you'll regret it," Jessica explained, hands on her hips.

"Like you haven't been doing that already? Telling people I don't clean the sinks?" Kim was furious, stepping toward her and standing her ground. Had the woman actually just threatened her like that? "Seriously? Use your words and tell me what your problem is."

Jessica just stood silent, her arms crossed and her face red. She was sucking her teeth, staring anywhere but Jessica's eyes, a sign of weakness that Malik had taught her was common in animal interactions and fights. Maybe Malik's advice was useful on more than just animals. Kim didn't *want* to fight with her. She had nothing against the woman prior to her treatment of Kim. Guilt would eat away at Kim later if she didn't at least try to understand why Jessica was doing this to her.

"I don't understand why you're hostile toward me," Kim finally said, her voice even and low. Another trick Malik had taught her when speaking to animals like his adorable mare, Hen. It already looked like Jessica was calming down. She wasn't blowing steam anymore and only stood there like a sullen child. "I would rather we just get along and help each other instead of this hostile relationship. I've never had anything against you, and I've never done anything to hurt you intentionally."

"Help each other?" Jessica scoffed, rolling her eyes. "Why would I want to help you? You're like this goddess and local celebrity and everyone acts like you're the only person around who can create and have worth. Why would I ever help someone like that?"

There it was. Was Jessica...jealous?

Kim stared at her with her mouth open, eyes wide. Jessica was shuffling her feet, as if realizing what she had just said and couldn't take it back. The shop eerily silent as the two contemplated the words that hung between them. Kim hadn't realized Jessica saw her through that lens. She had a good group of friends, did well at work, and got along well with people in town. Was that enough to make someone else jealous?

"I'm definitely not a celebrity," Kim pointed out. "And people treat me well because I'm nice and I work hard at my job. But Jessica, people talk about how well you do too when you're not around. You're really good at what you do, and I'm pretty good at what I do. It's not a competition. If anything, we could probably learn from each other to help each other's business."

Jessica glanced up at her from heavily mascaraed eyes. She looked wary but like an animal in the forest, maybe she was starting to trust. "People talk about my work?"

"Yes," Kim sighed in exasperation. "And maybe they would do it more often if you were nice to others once in a while. And there is no reason for you to keep sabotaging me. It's not like I'm taking any clients away from you. Like I said, we could be helping each other."

Jessica turned a little closer, more interested now. "How?"

Kim had not had enough tea for this conversation so early in the morning. If only they'd had this talk long ago. "I don't know," she said with a shrug. "I could help you with your braiding," she offered, voice still low. She wasn't sure if Jessica would go for it, but she had to try. As angry as she was about what Jessica had done, she would much prefer they were on friendly terms. "And maybe you could teach me to do manicures. I don't want to do that professionally, I love hair and braids, but I'd love to be able to do my own nails and maybe, one day, my kids'. You're truly a genius with gel manicures and I would be more than happy to exchange tips, tricks, and teachings if only we could be civil."

It was comical how much Jessica perked up. "You'd do that? You'd help me learn to braid?"

"Of course, we've known each other for years and I know

you'd be able to master them." Kim nodded, smiling softly now. "And since we do different services, we could be recommending each other to our clients. Like a duo-service." She exhaled a breath. "I've never done anything intentionally to hurt or cheat you, and I would much rather be friends than enemies. Or at least friendly co-workers."

"You aren't trying to use my skills or blackmail me over all this?" Jessica asked, stepping forward. "Truly?" What had this girl been through?

"I don't care about that; it's just product," Kim sighed, shaking her head. "I just think we could both be a lot happier if we just got along."

"You are really great at braiding," Jessica admitted, blushing slightly. In a matter of minutes, her entire demeanor had changed from hostile to open and smiling. "And you are so lucky to have a celebrity client. I'm so excited to meet her…"

Kim's day had changed drastically so early on. Thankfully, it was for the better and she found her mood the rest of the day to be ecstatic. The two of them chatted about the basics of braiding, the various forms of braids, and then Jessica showed her a few tips for putting on an even coat of nail polish before the shop opened. It was fun and Jessica became an entirely different person over the span of the conversation, eventually telling Kim about her job and life.

"I worked in retail before I finished my cosmetics training," Jessica explained, turning on the hot water kettle on the small counter and flipping on a few more lights. "One of the shift leaders was always trying to undermine me and made up stories to the boss about how I was stealing and using her to elevate myself to management. It was such a hassle and drama. I guess I just… never let that go and I've always approached things more cynically afterward."

"I can understand that, sounds awful." Kim nodded, grabbing some tea bags from her stash in her upper drawers. "I don't blame you for feeling the way you do or being cautious about people."

"I guess I've become the terrible co-worker, huh?"

Kim chuckled, shaking her head, and offering her a cup for the tea. She handed her a bag of the tea as well, both of them waiting silently for the small electric pot to warm the water. Kim could see Jessica was more at ease and they were both becoming content with one another.

"I think we're okay now." Kim nodded, pouring them both a cup when it was done. "We can teach one another, and all is forgiven. I like you already and I think we are going to be great co-workers, if not friends, in the future."

"You have to tell me where and how you found that man of yours," Jessica admitted, smirking. "I've heard so much gossip and stories that I'm ready to burst."

"Oh, well, perhaps we can dish a bit before everyone else gets here…"

"Please!" Jessica chuckled, raising her cup of tea. "To new beginnings?"

"To new friendships!"

CHAPTER TWENTY

"I'm so excited," Kim admitted, tying up her shoes. Her pack was sitting on his cabin's small porch, Malik checking his own pack for everything they needed. It had been more than a week since they had decided to climb the mountain and Malik was not feeling at ease.

It wasn't because of the weather, which was perfect, sunny, warm, with little rain or problems. It wasn't because the climb was difficult for beginners or that Kim wasn't a dedicated learner and had mastered the smaller cliffs around the cabin and at the sports complex. He was just uneasy about putting himself and Kim in danger. The thought of losing her, hurting her, or hurting himself, was frightening to him for the first time in his life and it made him terribly uneasy.

"The social media page has gotten quite a few likes and follows, and your videos are decently popular. Over ten-thousand views in the first week!" Kim explained, looking at her phone while she still had a bit of service. "The park even received two donations for their conservation fund, and they specifically mentioned your channel."

"Really?" Malik asked, surprised by this news. "Donations because of that video?"

"Yup. See, what did I tell you? Something simple, professional, and a bit fun gets attention and attracts people that want to help with conservation efforts."

"I guess I owe you an apology." He nodded, kissing her cheek and hoisting his bag over his shoulders. "You ready?"

"We won't vlog the climb," Kim explained, following him up the trail with her own pack over her shoulders. She put her cellphone in her deep jacket pocket, snapping it shut so it wouldn't be lost during the climb. "But we can before we start and after we reach the top."

"Your hair looks amazing." Malik smiled, reaching back to take her hand. "Is this the style you did for your celebrity client?"

"Oh, that was an amazing appointment but no, this is a different style I want to call Urban Climber. Something professional but also functional." She grimaced, squeezing his hand. "And I forgot to tell you some interesting news from the other day."

"You did?"

"Well, besides the celebrity client which was an amazing experience." Kim nodded, keeping up with him as they started the small incline to the next bluff and ridge. "I finally got somewhere with Jessica."

"Jessica?" Malik asked, shuffling around faces in his head. "Oh! That co-worker who doesn't like you. What's going on there?"

"Well, I walked in the morning my celebrity client was supposed to be there and Jessica was dumping my supplies," Kim explained, sounding exasperated. "I was so angry, livid, but then I remembered what you said, about keeping your head? Not letting emotions get the best of you in emotional situations."

"That's my girl." He nodded, smiling over his shoulder at her. "What happened? You report her?"

"No, no, something better happened." She nodded, letting go of his hand and following him up the steep incline. "We had it out, decided we'd be better off as colleagues and friends, and so I let her shadow me during my celebrity client's appointment."

"You did?" Malik asked, skeptical. "That's… generous."

"She's really kind and funny when you get to know her," Kim explained, breathing steadily as they mounted the top of the trail. "She agreed to teach me nails and I would teach her braids. Well, the client loved her braids, but Jessica also gained a commission. She wanted her nails done after seeing Jessica's amazing designs. It was a great day, truly."

"That's awesome!" he admitted, taking in one of his favorite views before continuing on up the hills and mountain ridge.

"The client even posted pictures on her massive social media pages." Kim smirked, sounding giddy. Malik smiled at this, enjoying her passions. "She even tagged and shouted us both on social. I'm booked for three months straight! And Jessica cannot keep up with the requests. It's amazing and just goes to show that anger and drama aren't always the way to go."

"I'm so proud of you." He smiled, wrapping his arm around her as they made their way up the winding rocky trail to the base of the mountain they'd hiked to last week. It wasn't too long of a hike but bordered the furthest edge of the park. "It all worked out and you made a new friend in the process."

"You've made tons of new friends lately," Kim pointed out, smiling at him as she followed up the trail. "Rochelle might be obsessed with you, the Zhang family wants to have us over for their next barbeque, and my granny is demanding a meeting for her annual peach blossom garden party."

"That sounds like a lot." He smirked, winking at her. "But I think I can do it. The real thing we should probably consider is living arrangements. I know you don't want me to leave the mountain because you think I'm sacrificing something but... I'd still be a ranger, you know? Able to come out to the cabin, maintain it, and maybe one day turn it into something for hikers, lodgers, or campers."

"Really?" she asked, shocked by his words. "You're interested in lodgers?"

"You can rent out cabins on the internet, yeah? Like a hotel?"

She chuckled, nodding in agreement. He seemed to have said something silly or cute because she wrapped her arms around him from behind, pausing at the top of another small hill where the trail started to switchback. He laughed, turning to hug her back before kissing her lips gently.

"So, what do you say? Maybe, if and when you're up for it, we can look for a place together with some space for my chickens and Hen?" He was a bit nervous asking her this, looking into her bright honey eyes as she contemplated his words. He could almost see the gears turning, her smile wide as she kissed his lips again.

"Absolutely, but let's wait until you meet my granny." She smirked, poking him. "Then you can decide if you still want to move in with me."

"Is your granny scary?" he asked, raising an eyebrow.

"She's very... particular and she has some high standards, especially for her eldest granddaughter." Kim winked, leading the way back up the trail. "Besides, I think it proper to meet a person's family before moving in with them, wouldn't you agree?"

"That is true," Malik surmised, following her with a nod. "So, what is this blossom party?"

It wasn't long until they were at the base of the mountain, another ten minutes, and a story about a party in the 1900s that was suspended for the war and the civil rights marches of the 60s. Kim's family had held one every year since the late 1890s and it was a social event that held meaning not only for her family but the community, as it marked a church massacre that occurred in 1891. Even though some of the history was dark, Kim's eyes lit up when she talked about Sweetgum and its past. He had never known someone to care so much about their community as she did.

Malik was fascinated with the local history, and when they got to the base of the cliff and got set up, he decided to highlight a bit of local native history in the video. He explained the name of the mountain, a few of the tribes who would call this place sacred, and he also explained the safety that was practiced when rock climbing. After demonstrating some basic ideas, Malik was ready to climb. He decided to lead the way, instructing her to watch where he grabbed, where he anchored, and the sturdiness of the rock. He knew she already knew this, but he was being extremely cautious.

She had already put away the camera, taking a few pictures with it of her hair and the scenery. The climb was tough, slow, but steady and Kim was doing great. She had taken her time, done exactly as he taught her, and was really coming into her comfort zone, eager to stay focused on the task at hand. He was happy she was enjoying herself too, talking to her as he climbed about his grandaddy's climbing stories and the snows of their mountain.

They reached a point where they could stop, a large ledge and outcrop of slick rock that needed to be crossed in order to get to the top. The divide was about three feet wide but wasn't overly difficult. Crossing it usually involved hoisting or propelling so Malik told her to be careful. It was a sharp fall of over ten feet onto a solid rock ledge and outcrop. An unlucky climber might even find themselves bouncing and breaking some limbs or their skull below. There had been accidents like that before, so Malik was prepared for the worse, his mind frenzied as he assessed the gap. It wasn't until he looked at Kim that he realized she wasn't looking at the divide but the view.

The view from atop that ridge was stunning, colors of all kinds shimmering at the edges of his vision. It was a very fine day, the sun twinkling over the treetops, lakes, and town below. It was distant, specks and shimmers in the breeze as they took in the scent and beauty of the world around them. Malik hadn't felt this proud and happy since his grandfather was alive.

Malik allowed Kim to cross over first, sinking an anchor into the rock and watching as she lowered and stretched across the gap. She was able to put one foot across, pulling herself over with her arms as she hoisted up toward the next rise where the peak of the cliff stood. Malik smiled at her as she stood on the other side, waiting patiently for him. He stepped across, using the same anchor point, hoisting himself to the far rock on the other side.

Before he could react, the rock below his foot shifted, his eyes wide as his stomach dropped milliseconds before he realized he was falling. The rush of air, the feeling of imbalance, freefall, and finally stunning pain in his leg and shoulder brought it all into stark relief. He was laying at the bottom of the divide, his shoulder burning and pulsing as his leg mimicked it. His breath had left his lungs in a sudden *woosh*, and now his chest heaved, desperate to regain the air. He could also hear the panicked gasp and cry of Kim as he fell, her voice above echoing around him.

"Malik!" she called, her strained voice making his mind race. He tried to move but pain lanced up the side of his body through the shock. He gasped and lay back down, unable to move.

"I'm all right, but I'm stuck!" he called up, keeping his cool. He knew that if she knew how bad it was, she'd panic and never be able to get through this. Panic was a person's worse enemy out here, in a place where improvisation was essential. "I think I might have fractured or broken my ankle; I can't tell!"

He was lying... he knew he'd broken his ankle, part of his foot, and his lower leg was clearly displaced. He didn't need her to know that, the pain in his shoulder reminding him of the time he dislocated his while hunting with his grandfather when he was thirteen. He didn't know how he was going to climb out of here, so he reached for his walkie with his other hand.

"I'm going to call down to the ranger station, stay put, don't panic!" Malik called up to her, hearing her soft cries.

"I can come down to you. I can pull you up..."

"No, no! Just wait, Kim, okay? I know you are afraid for me but please, take a deep breath," he instructed, looking through the dimly lit cavern for the walkie that was no longer in his utility belt or front jacket pocket. It was gone, his eyes roaming the dim shadows for anything that looked like the rectangular radio.

"I can't find the radio!" he admitted, hearing her voice from above.

"It's not up here!" she called, her voice steadying.

"It's dark down here, but I don't see it anywhere. It must have fallen below," Malik explained, his voice rising. "Listen, listen! You have to do exactly as I say, all right?"

"Anything!" she called back.

"Good, baby, good, then I need you to take a deep breath," he urged, looking up at the gap where she stood. He could see her standing as close to the edge as she dared. She was breathing heavily and had tears on her cheeks. He had to steel himself though, to be strong for her, so she could be strong for him.

"Okay, there you go, good," he encouraged, watching her shoulders heave with steady breaths. "Now, you're going to have to cross back over and climb back down alone. You need to get to the cabin and there is an extra walkie in the barn and in the cabin itself. Go call down to the ranger station like I showed you and explain to them that they need to get a rescue team up the mountain. Tell them I've fallen, broken my leg, and I need to be lifted out."

"I can't leave you alone!"

"You have to," he explained, nodding as best he could. "You hear me? You have to in order to get me out of here. You can do this, you hear? Slow and steady back down to the cabin, all right?"

There was silence for a moment, the wind whistling through the crag and around him as her sniffles disappeared. He then saw her nod, her voice steady and calm as she yelled back to him.

"I love you and I will bring back help," she stated, her resolve obvious.

"I know you do, and I know you will!" he called back, his voice wavering as she looked down at him. "I love you, Kim! Did you hear? I love you!"

"I hear you!" she called back, and before he could respond, she had nearly vaulted the gap above him, almost jumping across it as she regained her footing. She looked back at him, waving before reaching her hand out as if to take his. "I will be back, I promise! Don't worry, I can do this! I love you!"

Before he could respond she had disappeared, bag tight over her shoulder as the crunching of her steps disappeared. He laid there, alone in that cave and crag, thinking about two things. The pain was growing, aching, and burning while a stabbing sensation from his shoulder shot through him every time he took a deep breath. He knew he was injured and twisted laying at the bottom of this divide, but his mind wasn't primarily occupied with his safety.

Every moment that passed, every shadow that moved with the passing of the sun, he became more panicked. He feared that Kim could have fallen like he had, encountered a predator, hurt herself, couldn't find the way back, or was unsure how to use the radio. So many horrible scenarios went through his mind that he was making himself panic. He had to regain his composure, had to stay strong and trust that Kim was safe and able to contact the others. He just couldn't live with himself if anything happened to her. He loved her so much and, in his mind, he was begging whoever was listening to spare her, even if he couldn't be saved.

CHAPTER TWENTY-ONE

Kim was panicking inside, her body tight like a spring as she approached the edge of the cliff. Her pack was tight on her back and her mind was racing with scenarios. Malik could be dying, and she wouldn't even know it, unable to see him fully or to reach him. It was maddening and she hoped she could make it down the mountain in time to find him help before dark. The sun was starting to sink, and she didn't know how fast she could descend the cliff.

She took a deep breath, anchoring and hoisting herself down one ledge at a time. The slow, even descent was all she could think of, and her breathing was even as she dedicated every movement, every thought, and every reaction to her climb down that craggy rock-face. She never imagined she'd have to do this alone and the thought of Malik struggling made her heart ache.

Her heart was also pounding, her nerves fraught as she slowly grabbed one uneven surface after another. She was sure to sink her anchor, slowly repel, and make sure to always test her footing. She knew Malik's only chance to get out of there safely was if she reached the ranger station and his colleagues.

They could get him the help that she couldn't, and she needed them to know that it was an emergency. She needed them to understand what Malik meant to her.

He hadn't mentioned hitting his head, but she worried he did. A spinal and head injury up here would be impossible to treat and made worse with time. Her foot slipped at that moment, her hands grasping the ledge instinctually and cutting them as her foot dangled. She found another hold, regaining her composure and continuing the descent. It had frightened her, and she still wasn't quite half-way; she needed to focus and that's all that mattered. After making the hour long climb down the rock-face, over the first cliffs, and to the next ledge, Kim was exhausted. She had been going faster than they had climbed and the strain was making her arms and legs shake.

None of it mattered as she pressed on, climbing what felt like forever as she carefully tested her footing and hold. Soon after encountering a nest of bugs and a curious bird, she had reached the bottom of the cliff. Her legs were like jelly, her arms weak as she collapsed to her knees. It was tiring, her whole body aching and shaking as she tried desperately to get back up.

Once she was able to regain her feet, she discarded the ropes and some equipment, making her pack lighter so she could jog down the trail faster. She still had to be careful, descending down the bluffs and ledges to the forest below. It was another half hour or more hike down the trail and the sun was starting to sink. This caused shadows that Kim often mistook for creatures. That was the last thing she needed, her fears overrun by the fear that Malik could die alone here on this mountain, afraid and injured.

She pressed on, racing through the forest as the trees swayed above. It had to have been dinner time or shortly after, the long shadows dangling in the air as she finally recognized the trail around her. Only a few moments later and she'd be on the main trail to the cabin, only a short jog down the hill. It didn't take too long for her to reach the cabin, letting herself in. Kim was sweaty, hot, dirty, and desperate to find the extra walkie. Malik kept them atop the mantle at all times and she immediately switched it on, calling out for help.

"Come in, ranger station, this is Kim at the cabin," she called out, hoping this was the right channel. She knew there were certain channels they used, and this was the main one for the park communications.

"We copy, Kim, this is Lyle, switch to channel 32," he insisted, making her sigh as she switched over to the designated channel.

"Hello?"

"What's wrong?" Lyle asked, his voice full of concern and crackle over the radio.

"We were rock climbing up on the mountain, I insisted for videos and everything and Malik he... he fell," she said, her voice full of panic. "Lyle! He fell and I couldn't help him, and I just got back to the cabin, but he still needs help. He lost a walkie and it's getting dark... he said that he needs a rescue team, and he broke his ankle or leg."

"Deep breath!" Lyle commanded the moment she let off the button. "Stay at the cabin, the boys will be up shortly. I'll direct the rescue team once they get here. Do you hear me? Stay put and wait for them."

"I was the one who told him we should climb the mountain," she cried to him, losing her composure. "Lyle, he said I wasn't ready. He said we shouldn't, and I insisted. If he... I can't... "

"Hush now, girl," Lyle replied, his voice calm and soothing. "He'll be all right, I can promise you that. We'll get him out, but you need to stay strong, understand?"

"How? I love him..."

"The best thing you can do for someone you love is to support them, and that includes supporting the team who looks after them, all right? So, wait, take some deep breaths, and listen for the boys. They should be there sooner than usual. I've radioed them at the communications tower on the north ridge."

There was a pause, Kim waiting for further instructions as she sat on the step of the porch, bag still over her shoulders. She was a hot mess, and she didn't care, her tears streaming quietly as she waited for more news from Lyle. She needed to know Malik was okay and she wouldn't allow them to leave her behind.

"The boys will be there in ten minutes, they're on four-wheelers," Lyle crackled back, making her sigh in relief. "You wait for them, and I'll keep in touch about the rescue team. I've made contact so I've got to go. Stay there, Kim, you hear me? I know how you are… stay put."

"Yes sir," she crackled back, setting the walkie down and putting her head between her knees. She needed to calm down and be strong for Malik, Lyle was right, but she hated waiting and doing nothing.

It took everything in her not to go sprinting back up the mountain to Malik, and she hadn't realized how much time had passed but soon she could hear the revving of engines. Soon, two rangers came racing out of the woods, stopping with a sudden jerk, and cutting the engine. The two were the younger rangers who worked in Sweetgum, local boys with big hearts and sometimes small brains. However, today they looked like real rangers, both of them hopping off their vehicles to come inspect her.

"You okay?" Emry asked, eyes wide when he spotted her. He was the younger of the two.

"Any injuries?" Levi asked, looking her over. "What happened?"

Kim took her time explaining everything to them, the three concerned as they hadn't heard back from Lyle yet about the team. Levi was patient, waiting for word, but Emry and Kim were not in that kind of mood.

"We have to stay put and wait, or else the rescue team will never know where to go looking," Levi explained, checking his supplies. "Smoke flares don't work if it's dark, all right?"

"But we have to get to him before dark; he could be seriously injured," Kim pressured, looking at Emry for support.

"We could use the flare guns, take the walkie up the trail to the base of the cliffs at least," Emry offered, looking through the small supply crate on the four-wheeler. "We can setup an entry point at least, so the rescue team can spot us. He will need to be airlifted out."

"You heard the chief, no cowboy moves," Levi instructed, looking down at them both. "We need to rescue Malik, not endanger three more people in the process."

"At least let us go to the cliff so the helicopter knows where to be," Emry insisted, seeing Kim's outrage. "Come on, Levi. That isn't dangerous…"

"Fine, but you'll be the one taking the heat if Lyle comes down on us," Levi sighed, pinching the bridge of his nose. "Come on then, we'll radio down when we're there. Hop on with me, Kim."

The three of them had jumped onto the ATVs quickly after, Kim's arms tightly around Levi as they raced up the rough, uneven trail. They could only go so far on them, but it was closer to the cliffs than Kim had started earlier that day. It was a short hike up the last set of bluffs to where Kim had left the equipment and they wasted no time radioing down to Lyle their coordinates. Kim was panicking the whole time but, in her mind, she was begging that Malik's life be spared.

Unfortunately, as the sun was sinking, the clouds from the south and west were rolling in. She could feel the drop in pressure and smell the rain on the air, the panic overwhelming as both Levi and Emry debated what to do. Lyle's voice came over the radio a few minutes later, crackling in the air.

"The fire department is asking for the assistance of national guard helicopters," Lyle explained, Levi holding up the walkie. "The storm rolling in is leftovers from the hurricane in the gulf and it is making flying conditions hazardous. They expect at least two inches of rain so hold tight at the cabin until the team radios."

"We're not at the cabin, cap," Levi sighed, glaring at Emry. "We're at the base of the cliff, coordinates are being transmitted now."

"Where is Kim?"

"I'm here, Lyle, and I'm not turning back," she insisted, taking the walkie. "I won't be turned away or told to wait this out. I will be here for him when he is hauled off this mountain. Understand?"

There was a pause before Lyle responded, his voice defeated and full of worry. He consented but he made Levi and Emry swear that she wouldn't climb any further. That she'd wait for the choppers and the national guard. This she could do but she hated it, the rain falling slowly at first as they took shelter in the only safe spot on the mountainside, a small inlet under some overhanging rocks and branches.

CHAPTER TWENTY-TWO

The rain was falling softly as Malik lay there on the cold dark stone. It had been hours since Kim had left, and the worry had already driven him to tears and panic. The clouds had rolled in above with distant thunder and sprinkling mist before pouring steadily above. He wondered if she'd made it down the mountain, talking to himself out loud after a while. He needed to hear his own voice, needed those above to know he was still there, and he also had to get his thoughts out of his head.

He couldn't go fishing to banish his panic and worry, every moment bringing more stress as his shoulder ached and his broken leg and foot began to look bruised and red. He could picture Kim falling down the cliff, splitting her head open. He could see her being attacked by a mountain cat or a bear, mauled because he was too stupid to refuse her. He was too relaxed and wasn't paying attention to his own safety, and now Kim had paid for it.

She was probably dead on the rocks below the cliff, the rain falling on her beautiful face as she lay open to any animals to come along and take a bite. He had made himself sick with thoughts of how she could be hurt, alone, and afraid and ended up vomiting up his breakfast. It wasn't until then that he saw the pooling water in the small cave. The water from up top was cascading down the walls of the cave and filling the cavern where he lay. The water was already an inch high and growing, covering his clothes as they became heavy and unmanageable. He had managed to slip off his pack, hoisting himself with his good arm to and upright position.

However, now he could feel the roaring ache of his broken leg and knew for sure that at least one rib had been cracked or bruised. He sat in that cave, the tension rising as the water began to pool more quickly. The rain had picked up and soon the water was covering his legs and feet. He looked around at that point, wondering what he could do to get up higher, to another ledge or something. He didn't want to be weighed down by equipment, shedding everything but his knife and a rope so he could try and hoist himself higher with the rising water.

There was a single large rock that he could climb on top of, but it would be very difficult without use of his leg. He needed to figure out something as the water in that cave would rise, and soon, he might find himself drowning atop a mountain. After a few more minutes, water still rising, and a few fleeing muskrats, Malik tied the rope around himself, throwing the other end of the rope up over the shallow ledge a few feet above the rock.

He had to hoist himself up on top of it or within an hour he'd be drowned by the rising waters. That wasn't enough time for a rescue if Kim made it that far. The familiar pang in his chest had him breathing sharply out of his nose, deciding to focus solely on his survival until she returned. She had promised and he believed in her. So, he grit his teeth and grasped the rope with one hand. His shoulder was aching and stabbing as he used his other hand to try and secure himself.

It was painful, straining against the horrible shocks in his leg as he hoisted himself. He was able to lift himself above the rising surface of the water, swinging himself closer to the rock to try and pull himself up. Slipping more than once and falling back into the water, Malik didn't give up. His arm ached, his body was shaking, and he was weak and his eyes felt like lead, but he had to push through. If he didn't, he'd drown here and never be able to see Kim, or Lyle, or any of his newly made friends ever again.

He was struggling to grasp the rock, his shoulder screaming in pain as he grasped and slipped a few more times. The water was making it impossible but after another few minutes he made it up onto the boulder, hoisting himself roughly with the rope up to the top. He was above the surface of the water now, a good foot. However, it was rising fast, the dripping and trickling of rain from above reminding him that he wasn't out of danger. The water was still rising, and he had no guarantee that help was on the way.

He didn't want to lose hope but the thought of never holding Kim in his arms again was painful. He didn't want to leave her, not now when they'd found one another. He also didn't want to die alone like his grandaddy, something more frightening than he could admit. It was a desperate situation and he wanted more than anything to hear her voice, to see her face, and to kiss Kim one last time.

The thunder was rumbling above now, the rain pouring as the time seemed to creep by. What was probably minutes felt like hours and doubt started to creep into Malik's mind, followed shortly by a lurking insanity. He was near his limit, shivering and painfully wheezing as the rains above increased. He couldn't see anything now, the clouds obscuring any light that had been in the small cave cleft. Soon, he might be forever condemned to darkness, his body straining to cope with the shock of it all. There was a pressure in his stomach, something that he only experienced right before throwing up. If he did, it'd only make everything that much worse.

He was already out of energy, his stomach swirling and grinding in protest as he shut his eyes. He didn't think he'd hit his head earlier, but the exhaustion was getting to him, and he wanted more than anything to rest. He kept himself awake despite the lull of falling rain and rolling thunder, the trickling calm and soothing despite the desperate situation.

"I never got to meet her family," Malik sighed, speaking aloud now. He figured it couldn't hurt, his voice echoing with the thunder. "And I never got to talk to her granny or her other friends. I didn't get to go with her to the Founders celebrations or spend the holidays in her arms. I didn't even get a chance to ask her to be my wife."

The tears streamed down his cheeks like the rain, slow and painfully cold. He didn't know what to think, his mind reeling as he finally lost his nerve. Something in him was snapping, breaking under the pressure, and he desperately needed to see Kim again.

"Kim!" he called out, knowing she couldn't hear him. "Kim! Kim!"

Nothing but thunder, echoing drops of rain, and his own beating heart answered back.

CHAPTER TWENTY-THREE

"We can't just sit here while rain threatens rockslides, mudslides, and everything else," Emry argued, crossing his arms as the three stood huddled for shelter under the rock ridge. "The crevice could be filling with water as we speak."

"What?"

"Just quiet down," Levi sighed, shaking his head. "We can't make that climb in the rain. I won't do it; it's suicide."

"We have the rope, a folding gurney, and the equipment, so why not?" Emry asked, looking up at the cliff. "It isn't dark yet, we can still see, and the rain is letting up – the thunder and storms are moving off."

"We have to get up to him. He could need our help," Kim insisted, watching the swirling gray sky. "We can get up there within the hour if we try."

"Not in these conditions," Levi scoffed, rolling his eyes. "You aren't going anywhere. You are a novice, inexperienced, and will get yourself killed. Is that what you want Malik to find when he gets out of there? A dead girlfriend?"

"No but..."

"But nothing!" Levi sighed, dismissing Emry as well. "You two need to think about what you're saying and learn some patience."

"And if the rescue team can't get here for another hour or two? He'll be dead!" Kim spat, stepping away from him to grab up the equipment. "I don't care what you two do, but I'm going up there to help him. He needs to know I'm all right and that help is on the way!"

"You're crazy!" Levi yelled as Emry joined her.

"It's Malik!" Emry yelled back, shaking his head. "He's our friend… we have to try, Levi!"

Levi was silent for a moment, watching them closely before shrugging, agreeing to follow them up. He wasn't easy about this, but his sense of duty and loyalty was obviously overpowering his sense of safety. Kim was grateful for this, tying herself up in the drizzling rain as she hoisted herself up onto the first ledge. The climb was so slow, so dangerous, and harder than before. Kim ignored her screaming muscles, the slip of her foot, and the stiffness in her fingers as she climbed higher and higher.

The air was thin, and the thunder was distant, rumbling in the distance as she kept going. Emry and Levi were close behind, their calls and checks as they anchored themselves alongside her only making her heart pound more insistently. Levi hauled up the medical pack on his back, and Emry had the foldable gurney and rope tied securely to his back as he braved the slippery cliff. They had all forgotten about the crackling radio on Levi's hip as they ascended. Over an hour later, with exhausted gasps and shaking limbs, they made it to the ledge where Malik had fallen into the cave and divide.

Kim didn't hesitate, crawling over to the opening to hear her name being called out, faint at first but growing louder. She was so relieved to hear his voice that she called back over the thunder and rain.

"Malik! Malik, we're here!"

Kim was horrified to see that the thin cave was filling with water. She couldn't see Malik very well, but he had managed to raise himself up onto a higher surface. The water was still rising, covering parts of his legs and hips. He looked tired, sick, and afraid, but she yelled out to him again so he could hear, his eyes finding hers gratefully.

"Hold on! Emry has a gurney! You'll be out soon!"

"Even if Emry is able to lower himself down there," Levi hissed, trying not to be too loud. "It doesn't guarantee he can hoist him out. There's also nowhere to put him once he is hoisted up. I don't think you and I can pull him up by ourselves…"

"Then lower me. I'll get him on the board and you two can lift," Kim insisted, moving to start lowering herself down in.

"She's lighter and we can pull them both back up," Emry said, keeping her back from the crevice as he crossed it to lower down the gurney. "We'll stay up here and when you give the signal, we'll pull as hard as we can."

"Don't drop us," Kim warned, grimacing slightly as she tied herself up tight with the ropes and pulleys Levi was setting up. "I'll be back up in a flash with Malik so make sure you radio down to the station."

"Yes, ma'am," Emry nodded with encouragement, looking down into the crevice. "How you doing down there, Malik?!"

"Get me out of here, you idiot!" Malik yelled back, all three of them grinning.

"Here I come!" Kim yelled down.

"No! Do not send her down here! Are you crazy?!"

"We need to move fast, Malik," Kim argued, speaking over Levi. "This is the best option so quiet down and get ready to be rescued!"

They slowly lowered her, and she was relieved to see it was all holding tightly. There was no give, and both the boys were steady with the rope as she was lowered slowly down the divide.

When she finally could see Malik, she realized the water was higher, almost to his chest. He was shivering and looked exhausted, watching her with worry as she came closer.

"Almost there, baby." Kim smiled, reaching out to him. He was only able to lift one arm and she held back a sob as she was finally able to touch him. She instinctively grabbed for him, pulling desperately so he was out of the water, but he didn't move very far. The gurney was right behind her, Kim electing to float in the small space as she insisted on lifting Malik as best she could onto the small but sturdy gurney.

"The water is rising!" Kim yelled up, flailing as Malik was finally able to sit squarely on the board. He was able to pull himself up with one arm and she helped him as she floated in the cold rainwater. "Pull him up! GO!"

"Don't leave her behind!" Malik yelled, the rope straining as he was hoisted, one jarring foot at a time, further from Kim who was floating in the rising water. She was reaching toward him as he rose out of the gap, disappearing over the edge.

In that moment she was alone, flailing, and sinking as the rope started dragging her down now. She screamed out but was pulled down, desperate to grab onto the rope again to pull herself out of the now swirling and crushing rush of water around her. She couldn't hear anything but that deafening rush, and before she could react, her mouth and lungs were full of burning and gritty water. She flailed in the waves and was trying desperately to find her way up to the surface.

It was then that the rope went tight, and the water started to move away from her. Soon, cool burning air hitting her lungs in gasps. She could barely hear Malik's panicked voice over the patter of rain, the rush of the crevice below, and the echo of the mountains around her. She was shivering, clinging to the rope, when she felt a pair of hands hoist her up and into their arms. Malik was there, holding her as he sat atop the gurney, his eyes wide in fear.

"Kim!" he yelled, wincing as he embraced her the moment she was within reach. "Kim! You're safe, oh God…"

"Not quite," she sputtered, holding him in a wet embrace. "We have to get out of here." Even as she said it, relief washed through her now that Malik was in her arms. The hard part was done and help was coming.

"I was so worried," he replied, holding her desperately, as if she'd float away. "Are you okay? I thought I'd never see you again."

His lips found hers and, in the rain, they kissed, holding one another as best they could. Both Levi and Emry were nearby, pretending not to notice their embrace as they kissed and whispered sweet nothings to one another.

"I was worried about you too," she whispered, stroking his chin gently, inspecting his face lovingly. "I was so worried, Malik. I can't imagine losing you…"

"I love you," he breathed, kissing her cheeks and lips gently. "I love you."

"I love you, too… oh, I love you, too."

EPILOGUE

ONE YEAR LATER

alik and Kim snuggled together under a plush blanket. The fire roared before them as they sat close in their foldable sling chairs. They had arrived at Grand Canyon National Park only a few days ago, but it had been a year since Malik's fall and their harrowing climb. A lot had happened since then, but it was all good things. Kim pondered their journey as they enjoyed their small desert fire alongside their small RV. They'd been traveling for the past month across the U.S. visiting all the national parks and landmarks of the south and southwest.

They'd head north soon, but for now, their beautiful view of the sunset, stars, and the canyon below made her heart soar with happiness. This was what she needed, and she was grateful that they had the opportunity to enjoy one another like they did. She was as content as a cat, and a soft sigh escaped her lips as she took in the fading red sun over the orange, purple, and navy skyline dotted with stars.

"What are you thinking?" Malik asked, kissing the top of her head as she leaned against his shoulder. His presence was something she didn't dare take for granted.

"Everything." She nodded, holding him close. "Our lives, what we've been through, and how grateful I am to have you."

"It was a pretty dangerous courtship, wasn't it?" he asked, glancing down at her with a sly smile. "I thought I'd be in that cast forever."

"It was only a couple months, and it was quite a learning experience for me," she pointed out, kissing his cheek. "I got to stay with you for two months and learn all there was to know about taking care of dear Hen."

"I hope she isn't missing us too much," he sighed, his eyes lost in the fire.

"She's happy with Lyle and the boys," she assured, squeezing his arm. "And we'll be back soon to find her a permanent pasture to enjoy. Okay?"

"I still feel bad for uprooting you like this…"

"No, it was my choice to come along," she assured, watching the fire as well. "Besides, it is working out beautifully. We'll be back in Georgia in less than a year and the pop-up shops I've been advertising on social media for my braids have been amazing. I'm booked the next three weeks in California, Oregon, and Washington."

"Glad to hear it, my love," he whispered, kissing her forehead gently, his lips grazing her cheek as they found her own lips.

"Putting our location on Instagram and using the RV has been pretty successful." She smirked, lacing her fingers with his. "I'm so glad we could do this together. Seeing all the National Parks was a brilliant idea, love."

"Well, I had a lot of paid vacation, so Lyle is being quite generous," he assured her, squeezing her hand in his as he pulled back a little to look down at her. His dark eyes were always so fiery, burning for her as he gently stroked her cheek with his other fingers. "It couldn't have worked out better."

"Anywhere and any time I'm with you is perfect," she sighed, blushing as he smiled down at her. She didn't care that she sounded all lovey-dovey. There was nowhere else in the world that she would rather be right now.

"Oh, so maybe I shouldn't do this then…"

Before she could react, he pulled the blanket off, and dropped to one knee. Her heart jolted as she realized what he was about to do. While keeping his eyes on her, he pulled out a small black box.

Time seemed to stand still as she stared at the box, their eyes meeting as he opened it. Inside was a beautiful but simple gold band ring with a small diamond in the center. Flanking it looked like two small flowers made of emeralds and amethyst. She couldn't believe how beautiful the ring was as tears came streaming down her cheeks.

"Don't cry, my love," he whispered, as he knelt before her. "But Kimberly Thena Wright, will you marry me?"

"Yes!" she practically screamed, tackling him to the dirt with frantic kisses and desperate fingers. She was so happy, unable to control herself as they both snuggled up in the dirt together, and he slipped the ring on her finger with a laugh. It was an unbelievable night, the stars twinkling above as they both held one another near that crackling, warm fire.

AUTHOR'S NOTE

I am deeply honored that you took the time to read Love Between Us, the first book in Sweetgum Meadows Romance series of stand-alone novels. If you enjoyed this book, please consider leaving it a review so that others may find it as well.

If you enjoyed reading Kim and Malik's story, make sure you check out their FREE bonus scene here, where Malik meets her family:

https://swiy.co/LBU-Bonus-Scene

I look forward to introducing you to the other characters in this lovely, family-oriented town where each couple will find their happily ever after.

You can get the next books in the series by visiting ImaniPrice.com.

ALSO BY IMANI PRICE

Book 1: Love Between Us

Book 2: Sweet Sunsets

Book 3: Infinite Kiss

Book 4: Dance With Me

Book 5: In Charge

Book 6: Forever With You

Book 7: Secret Sweethearts

Book 8: Endless Love

Book 9: The Harder We Fall

Book 10: Reservations of the Heart

Book 11: Play by Play

Book 12: Guarded Hearts

Book 13: Healing Hearts

Book 14: Dear Sweetgum

Book 15: Lanterns of the Meadows (novella)

Book 16: Drawn to You

Book 17: Under the Sweetgum Tree

Sweetgum Meadows' Visitor's Guide

My full audiobook catalog is available for FREE on YouTube. Check
it out here: https://swiy.co/Sweetgum

To all my lovely readers,

Thank you
for
reading